Stella Whitelaw has ha[...]
national magazines. In [...]
London Magazine 'The [...]
tion judged by Sheridan [...]
beautiful cats who give her endless inspiration and pleasure.

By the same author

Cat Stories
More Cat Stories
True Cat Stories
Grimalkin's Tales (with Judy Gardiner and Mark Ronson)
New Cat Stories
Collected Cat Stories (omnibus edition)

Stella Whitelaw

THE OWL AND
THE PUSSYCATS

Grafton
An Imprint of HarperCollinsPublishers

HarperCollins*Publishers*
77–85 Fulham Palace Road,
Hammersmith, London W6 8JB

A Paperback Original 1993
1 3 5 7 9 8 6 4 2

'Glad Tidings' first published in *Active Life* 1992
'Something Funny in the Attic' first published in
Woman's Weekly 1989
'The Fox' first published in *Woman's Realm* 1987
'Topper' first published in *Woman's Weekly* 1987
'Prickly Lady' first published in *Woman's Weekly* 1988

A catalogue record for this book is
available from the British Library

ISBN 0 586 21528 X

Set in Linotron Janson

Printed in Great Britain by
HarperCollinsManufacturing Glasgow

CONTENTS

To Janice,
who likes owls

Do not expect me to be your slave, I have a thirst for
  freedom.
Do not probe my secret thoughts, I have a love of mystery.
Do not smother me with caresses, I have a preference for
  reserve.
Do not humiliate me, I have a sense of pride.
Do not, I beg, abandon me, I have a sure fidelity.
I'll return your love for me,
I have a sense of true devotion.

Belgian traditional poem

SEA CAT

Curnock Bay was used to seeing the cat swimming. The tourists weren't. They got out their cameras and videos, dodging about the sandy cove, clambering over rocks, hoping their candid shots would get on to a television programme.

The cat swam from rock to rock, his dark head like an otter, barely visible against the waves, held high because he disliked water in his eyes or up his nose. But he loved the sea: he loved the waves, the foaming white horses, chasing sand crabs into the sea, playing tag with the oncoming tide.

Joe did not call his cat Rocky because of this strange habit of swimming. The name came from his admiration for the cat's sense of survival. They lived together in a stone-walled cottage near the harbour where Joe's fishing boat was tied up. He caught mackerel for a living.

He'd found the stray tabby kitten one stormy night, drenched and bedraggled as the sea lashed the harbour wall and spilt its fury wetly over the walkway. He saw this tiny dark object swirling round in the ebbing water and thought it was a dead bird. Then he realized it was a grey striped kitten, and only half dead.

The kitten went home tucked inside his fisherman's jersey, as much comforted by the warmth of Joe's body as by the strong fishy smell. A creature that smelt good enough to eat must be worth knowing.

The swimming came about by accident. Rocky hated being left behind when Joe took his boat out to go fishing. He sat on the quay, meowing and calling, pacing up and down on the slippery edge. Joe swore that the cat sat there for hours, just waiting for him to return. It worried him that the cat might fall in the harbour and drown.

'Why don't you bring that daft cat of yours with us then?' said one of his crew. 'As a mascot, like.'

Rocky needed no encouragement. He followed Joe aboard, tail aloft, on jaunty sea-paws, soon found his way about, and – more importantly – soon discovered when to keep out of the way. He kept out of the noisy engine room and took refuge in the galley when they were hauling in the brimming nets. He knew his share of the fish would come later.

The crew liked having him around. He was affectionate, purred a lot without fawning. He sat for hours, eyes closed and sunning himself, or curled up fast asleep in some warm spot. He sharpened his claws on the mast and learned to walk precariously along the gunwale. If the weather was bad he went below or installed himself in Joe's wheelhouse, watching the instruments that gave Joe guidance to bring the boat safely home.

He was always the first ashore. It was a standing joke. He barely waited for the rubber bumpers to nudge the sea wall before leaping on to the walkway.

'That cat'll fall in one day.'

And Rocky did. He misjudged the jump as the boat rocked backwards on the tide. His claws scraped wildly at the edge of the cement wall. It was too wet and slippery for any purchase. Rocky fell twenty feet into the murky harbour water.

Joe's first reaction was to leap for a lifebelt, then he realized that was stupid. He peered over the side of the boat, already ripping off his big boots and jersey. There was nothing for it but to go in after his pet.

'Damned cat,' he swore, knowing the water would be cold and unpleasant. Although the harbour was washed out by the tides, it always had a stale and stagnant smell, and anything could be down there . . . including a drowned cat.

'Hold on, guv! There's summit moving.'

Rocky was not only moving, Rocky was swimming. He was striking out with a splashy dog-paddle, fuelled by fear and determination. And he was not disorientated by the fall and unexpected plunge down into the depths. He was heading for the the slimy green steps at the end of the habour.

'My God, that cat's swimming . . .' Joe pulled his boots back on, jumped ashore and hurried to the end of the harbour wall, shouting words of encouragement to his cat valiantly swimming below. 'Come on, Rocky. You can make it. Come on, Rocky my lad . . .'

The steps were slippery and lethal but Joe gripped on to the verdigris-coated rail as he climbed down. Rocky was exhausted. Joe leaned down and hauled the bedraggled cat out of the water.

'Well, you're a rum 'un. I thought you were a gonner.'

Rocky choked. The water tasted absolutely foul; nothing like the fresh salty spray that covered the deck of the fishing boat. He was relieved to be on dry ground but at the same time his mind registered a certain lively curiosity.

He took to following Joe on his daily walks along the cove. Sometimes it was an early morning walk, sometimes late in the evening when the dusk turned the sand to grey and the waves deepened to indigo. He played tag with the breaking wavelets, often getting his paws wet and his long striped tail soaked. He did not seem at all afraid.

He saw a seagull bobbing cheekily on the waves and plunged in, paddling fiercely. The bird screeched in dismay and rose into the air, wings flapping. Rocky hardly seemed to notice. He had discovered swimming. He swam to a nearby rock and climbed out, shaking his fur like a disgruntled seal. But he wasn't angry. He was serenely satisfied.

From that moment, there was no stopping Rocky. He was in the sea at every opportunity. The cove was his personal playground. He combed the beach for creatures to chase into the sea, surprised the summer visitors with his expertise in the water, wished he had a friend to play with in the tantalizing waves.

One afternoon a maverick bottle-nosed dolphin appeared in the cove. It was spotted by the crews of several fishing vessels, ploughing and diving, completely alone. Dolphins had been seen before, some years earlier, cavorting in the warmer water of the Southwest coast beyond Curnock

Cove. But this one was alone. The locals were afraid it was going to beach itself, die in the shallows.

Crowds gathered on the cliff above the cove, watching the beautiful creature diving and splashing, its long body gleaming like grey steel, hearing its distressed whistle above the calls of the gulls and cormorants.

'It's coming ashore,' said Joe sadly. 'Like a whale. Its echo-location is upset. We'd better get down there and see if we can persuade it to return to deeper water.'

Rocky followed his master down into the cove. He too had seen the dolphin and was fascinated by its size and agility in the water.

The whistles from the dolphin's blowhole were high-pitched and plaintive. Rocky's ears perked, whiskers twitched. He did not understand what the dolphin's whistles meant, but his senses were alert to the tone. The dolphin was clearly calling for help.

If a dolphin could look depressed, then this dolphin did. Its eyes were lacking lustre, its expression wounded. It glided mournfully towards the shore, drawn by some inescapable fate.

Some of the men began to wade into the shallows, splashing and beating the water. Rocky streaked between them, racing through the wavelets, heading straight for the dolphin. He struck out, his paws paddling the water like waterwheels, water streaming from his body.

He reached the dolphin and splashed around it. It seemed to take no notice. Rocky climbed out on to a rock and shook himself, then he dived back into the sea, closer now, circling, hoping it would play. The dolphin rolled over to look at this odd little creature.

Rocky raced away, taunting the dolphin to a chase. The

dolphin tried to turn, intrigued, its dome-shaped head well above the water, long tail thrashing the shallows. It was already almost too late. Rocky pranced through the water, flinging crystal droplets in all directions. He wanted to play, knowing it would be fun. This big animal had more sense than those stupid birds. The disparity in size was immaterial. It made little difference in the water.

The dolphin's whistle was weaker but its headlong plunges towards the shore had been halted. It seemed uncertain of what to do. The men were also flummoxed.

'We'll get some nets,' said Joe. 'Rocky ... come on, Rocky. You can't do anything.'

But Rocky was not giving up so easily. He sat on a rock, panting, aware now that the dolphin was eyeing him and there was a glimmer of interest. Rocky ran along the crest of the ridge, to the deeper water. He had never swum in such deep water before but he showed no fear.

He struck out, again daring the dolphin to chase him. The dolphin began a high click-click noise, tentatively at first. A big wave came and shifted his smooth flank. Rocky's excitement was instinctive; he was following a dream. The dolphin seemed to perk up as another wave took him a few feet further out.

'The tide's going out,' said Joe tensely. 'It might just move the dolphin out into deeper water.'

The dolphin put his head above the waves to see what that cat was doing now. There was something so appealing about the creature's crazy antics in the water. His big flipper tail flapped in appreciation.

Joe could not believe what his eyes were telling him. The dolphin was plunging towards the cat, movements huge and graceful. Rocky was delighted. There was no fear or sense of menace. Minutes later they were splashing and romping like two old friends.

It was Rocky who gave up first. He was tiring and he wanted his supper. The dolphin seemed to understand and blew whistles from his blowhole as the cat went ashore to where Joe stood, amazed.

The next morning Rocky could not wait to get down to Curnock Cove. The dolphin was waiting, his short beak opening to a big smile. He blew a whistle of welcome as the cat climbed along the rocks to the deeper water. They played all day. People came to watch. The television cameras arrived. In the following days pleasure boats were putting out carrying tourists and summer visitors, everyone hoping to catch a glimpse of the cat and the dolphin.

Joe was furious. 'You'll kill them both with your stupid sight-seeing,' he shouted, shaking his fists. 'Can't you leave 'em alone?'

The dolphin was worried for his new friend. They were playing in deeper and deeper water and the cat, who seemed to have no fear, had further and further to swim back to shore.

One morning when Rocky went down to the cove the dolphin had gone. The cat combed the beach, looking out to sea for any trace of the big creature, listening for that familiar whistle or clicking. Rocky sat very still for a while, like an extension of the rocky edge, then slowly went back to the harbour. He sensed that the dolphin had gone to look for the rest of his family group.

'Come along, old fella,' said Joe from the deck of his boat. 'Your friend has gone.'

*

The cat went back to his old routine on the fishing boat. He soaked up the sun, totally at home as the vessel rode the troughs of water in the fishing grounds. His coat became beautifully glossy as he grew to maturity. He sired several litters of kittens ashore, each carrying his distinctive grey stripes.

The fishing was nearly over for the day, the sun going down. The haul had been heavy and the crew were hosing down the decks. Rocky sat up, alert, stretching his neck. He had heard something. He moved cautiously along the slippery deck, keeping out of the way of the hose.

Far away his keen eyesight saw a group of dolphins leaping in the air, checking the whereabouts of hunting sea birds which would show them where to find the fish shoals. Rocky spotted a familiar sleek grey body plunging through the water, making straight for the fishing boat. Rocky jumped up on to a pile of rope to get a better view, his whole body quivering.

Moments later he was paddling madly in the sea to meet his friend. The dolphin blew triumphant whistles, leaping even higher in joy. They played and romped in the water, oblivious to all the activity going on in the boat. Sometimes the crew saw the cat clinging to the back of the dolphin, having a ride, resting.

The engines stopped. Joe threw a rope ladder over the gunwale and climbed down, swearing. 'You damned cat,' he called, but there was no anger in his voice. 'I'll be lucky if I don't get a ducking. Rocky, come here.'

The cat saw his master and swam towards him. He scrambled up on to Joe's shoulder and clung there as Joe climbed back up on to the deck. The dolphin dived away skittishly, showing off, obviously delighted to have found Rocky again.

The engines started up and the boat turned towards the land, followed for a while by the dolphin playing in the bubbles of the wash. Then the creature made a final graceful lunge and swam away.

'Don't think I'm going to do this every day for you,' said Joe, grumbling, pulling up the rope ladder.

But, of course, he did.

And Rocky swam often with his friend, fished with Joe, followed the life he wanted to lead, a cat of a different breed.

A cat that could swim.

ESCAMILLO

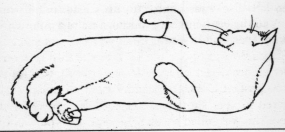

*E*scamillo could draw blood. It was a skill of which he was immensely proud. Yet he looked so gentle and affection-ate. He had the squashed ruffed face of a reformed angel with tawny jewelled eyes and thick, dense sandy-grey fur with white underparts. His ears stood up with long black tufts. He was big but still managed to sit on a victim's lap, like a colossal cushion, with throbbing purrs and innocent stares, then wham! He dug all eighteen claws simultaneously into a plump knee or thigh with the accuracy of a dentist's drill.

It always drew blood. Escamillo smirked. He loved the shrieks, the cries, the shock of tears, the pandemonium. It pleased the ham actor in him. It was his little drama for the day, totally unscripted, unpredictable in sequence, but always wholly satisfactory. He was not named after a famous matador for nothing.

'You'll have to get rid of zat cat, darling,' wept Elizabeth Brumhold, one of Conchita's friends, dabbing at her wounded knees. 'He's a menace ... but why? He knows me so well. I was doing nothing, absolutely nothing, just stroking him, when he dug all his claws into me. It's very unnerving.'

'Gorgeous darling,' said Conchita, burying her fingers deep into Escamillo's thick fur. 'It's his way of protecting me. You're a naughty boy; you mustn't hurt your Mummy's dearest friend, even if you think you are protecting me.'

Escamillo pawed ecstatically into the fluff of Conchita's pearl embroidered jumper. It was true. It was his role in life to protect Conchita Sanatini from all things small and covered in very short fur. She took him to every theatre where she was billed to sing. In fact, she would not sign a contract until he had given the theatre a clean bill of health.

'You know I can't stand anything creepy-crawly ... mice, bats, spiders, woodlice, beetles, ants, daddy-longlegs or any such horrid things,' she went on. 'Escamillo is a brilliant hunter, such high climbing and jumping. I can't perform if I think there's a mouse around. My voice simply goes. It's extraordinary.'

'How extraordinary,' Elizabeth drawled. 'My voice never goes. Nothing can disturb it.'

'Solid as a rock, as always,' said Conchita with a disarming smile. She knew she could sing Elizabeth off any stage. She had power, range and a fluid delivery; she could hit a top C like a silver tuning fork. But Conchita refused to admit that she could not act. On stage, even the scenery had more life.

Elizabeth could act. She could summon any emotion from

one to ten. And from a distance, she looked good. But the voice . . . it was pure and dramatic, yet smaller.

The two opera stars had been friends for years, but the public friendship walked a narrow path strewn with detonators. They met with claws sheathed, fangs withdrawn, poison darts hidden in handbags.

Both Conchita and Elizabeth were top opera singers. They sang all over the world in famous opera houses, vying each other for the big roles. But they were as different as Pavarotti and Domingo. Conchita always had the edge over Elizabeth; she had the voice, the presence, and off-stage acting that was streets ahead of what she produced on stage. But she sang without heart, some said. Elizabeth's voice had the emotion and she could act . . . opera buffs argued for hours on their merits.

'Darling,' said Conchita. 'You're not still mad about Budapest, are you? Truly, it was a fluke that I got the part. You were so much better than I. Even I say so.'

'Then how come zat you got the role?'

'A mystery . . . fate perhaps. I was so upset for you.'

Elizabeth did not believe her. Conchita did not know how to be upset for anyone. There had been something very fishy about Budapest but Elizabeth doubted if she would ever find out how fishy. A whale-size mystery, if she knew Conchita.

'How kind,' said Elizabeth. 'But I'm sure to get the Festival Opera Season in Sussex. After all, country theatres suit me. And the natural lighting is excellent for my skin. It just glows.'

'Ah, make-up is so wonderful these days . . .'

Escamillo yawned, a trifle bored. He'd been dreaming of open spaces and running wild. He wondered if it was time for a repeat performance. He surveyed local laps and declined all offers. He had to keep his strength up in case he had a theatre to vet. He stretched his front paws, arching his back into a high curve. Then he shook out his fur and moistened his eyes.

'Who's so big and beautiful?' cried Conchita, scooping him up into her powerful arms. 'Who's a darling? Who's mumsie's gorgeous pet?'

He purred on cue into her ear, wet nose and all. She was up to something. He could tell. All that sweetness and light. It was not normal. He had not shared Conchita's career for six years without learning a trick or two.

Elizabeth did get the prestigious Festival Opera. She could not wait to rush round and tell Conchita. She would be singing Electra, Greek princess and the high priestess in Mozart's *Idomeneo*, the vengeful soprano whose great tirade of hate against her rival would tax any voice. It was a part that required dramatic acting, especially in the cave scene which climaxed in a series of scale passages very like high screams.

'Congratulations, darling,' Conchita raved. 'You will be able to scream so beautifully. You have the hardness of tone that the role demands. It does not require a singer to scream. You will suit the role admirably.'

'Thank you, darling. You are such a marvellous friend.'

Escamillo was thankful he did not have to prowl yet another theatre, especially one in the country. He hated all the cobwebs and dead insects that clung to his fur and his whiskers. He much preferred watching the television and going for walks in the park on his cream and gilt-studded leather lead. People stared so. His ego soared. He was perfecting how to cross his eyes.

Afterwards he was not quite sure which event followed which. He knew Elizabeth was good as Electra because Conchita had told him so through clenched teeth. He knew the first night was a great success and she got rave reviews. Conchita was furious.

'But she can't sing,' Conchita wailed. 'How could she be so wonderful with a voice like a ripsaw? The critics must be deaf, deaf as poles. They are all foolish apes. I would have sung superbly!'

Escamillo poured sympathy into her ear. He knew who fed him gourmet food; he was not stupid. Nor was he deaf. Conchita began singing Electra day and night. She was familiar with the role. It was not a good sign. He crept under a table and buried his head in a flank of fur to shut out the noise. When God made him an opera singer's cat, He should at least have given him a musical ear.

Escamillo was head first under the duvet one afternoon when he was abruptly awoken by a thousand notes coming from the music room. Conchita was rehearsing Electra! Seriously! The voice was ecstatic with triumph.

'Elizabeth is ill! She has a throat infection! She cannot sing. I shall offer my services immediately. I am ready to go. This is my moment. I have never sung at the Festival Opera . . .'

Conchita was waving the day's newspaper like a fan, her hair coming loose in her excitement.

'Escamillo, where are you? I must phone my agent. We must be ready to leave in an hour. I shall need a run through with Sir George today, then a walk through in the morning. Oh, the honour, the prestige . . . royalty will be present, the aristocracy . . . champagne on the lawns in the interval . . . all so beautiful. It will be the crown of my career.'

The management of the Festival Opera was naturally delighted by Conchita's offer since Elizabeth Brumhold was indisposed. They sent a limousine for her.

'Come, my pet, and get into your basket. We are going to Sussex. Now the audience will hear real singing!'

Escamillo stifled a yawning sigh. Another theatre. Reluctantly he jumped into his designer basket. It was the fanciest cat basket in the world, upholstered inside and out. But the real glory was the suit of lights, glittering with coloured glass and sequins, the toreador's glorious bolero of courage. The bolero was draped in all its magnificence as a cover over Escamillo's basket, hanging like a banner, his badge of office.

The Festival Opera Season was held annually in the heart of Sussex. They drove through leafy lanes and over wooded highwayman heaths towards the Sussex manor house that played host to this great event. The theatre had been built in the grounds, among spacious lawns and flower gardens. A long lake serpentined its way through the weeping trees like a pale ribbon of glass.

'Here we are, Escamillo. I'm taking you straight to the theatre and you can have a good sniff round. Do it well, precious cat, for I must sing my best!'

Conchita was well known for this idiosyncracy throughout the theatrical world. It was tolerated with asides and grins from the backstage staff. She took Escamillo round all the nooks and crannies on his lead and then, when he was familiar with the layout, she let him off the lead.

Escamillo reverted to his origins in the Old World, ancient genes racing. It was like drawing blood only more exciting. He created mayhem, a long hiss coming from his jaws. The stage crew backed off, alarmed. They had never seen a cat quite like Escamillo. The massacre was medieval, bodies hacked to pieces, wings, tails, whiskers flying in all directions. When he had finished, he sat back and licked down his fur, made a studied and fastidious grooming of every displaced hair.

'Strewth,' gasped the stage manager. 'Somebody's got to clear this lot up. Bert!'

Escamillo smirked modestly and wandered off for his supper. He never ate the things. Ergh . . . raw, unfilleted, too uncouth for his taste. He preferred a nice piece of smoked haddock with a soupçon of cream.

Conchita's rehearsal and walk through went without a hitch. She was a static actress, so the walk was barely a stroll.

It was a beautiful summer's evening with a breeze as soft as gossamer. The grounds were full of beautiful women wandering about in long, floaty dresses, and well-walleted men in dinner jackets. They drank champagne from goblets and parked their Fortnum and Mason hampers in secluded spots, with a tartan rug to mark their territorial rights. The popping of champagne corks added to the growing excitement as the audience filed into their seats.

Behind the safety curtain, the stagehands made their last checks on the scenery. The singers stood in distracted solitude, each concentrating on their own method of relaxing, of coming together, of coping with nerves, line-loss, their own incredible insecurity and lack of confidence.

Only Conchita, it seemed, was without nerves that evening. She stood, all powerful, a dominating figure in her flowing gown of white and gold. She was going on that stage to do what she did best, sing! Elizabeth Brumhold would be in the audience and she was going to get a lesson in real singing.

Conchita sang divinely. Every note flowed. The critics tormented their brains for new words to describe the perfection of her voice. She was giving her all and to hell with the acting. The audience closed their eyes and simply listened to her voice.

Escamillo yawned in his basket. He had heard it all before. He dreamed of escaping, of going home . . .

The interval came and went in a flurry of more popping champagne corks, smoked salmon and river trout, duckling and caviar, strawberries and cream. Conchita basked in her dressing-room, sipping a little honey and water.

'I am like a flower,' she said to her mirror image, holding the glass aloft. 'I need only the nectar of the gods.'

The opera continued well. There was no doubt that Conchita's performance was going to be a triumph. Her voice took on a new, magnificent dimension.

There was always one spot on the stage where the voice was sure to resonate with greater sharpness, intensity and volume. Conchita, with her unerring professionalism, had found the place. She stood, stately as a statue, as the stage-lights dimmed to the darkness of the cave set. The spotlights were on her alone and she was ready for the final cadenza which would end in the great dramatic scream.

The subterranean and rocky set was eerie with gloom and doom. The audience shivered.

Conchita was not affected by the atmosphere. As an actress she should have been, but her more practical reaction was a passing dismay in case her face was not properly lit.

As she sang, it got darker. She had an uncanny feeling she was not alone.

Whoosh. Whoosh.

There was a slight movement through the air. Another

brief displacement, dark, fast, occurred across the stage. It was difficult to see. First it was there, then it wasn't.

Whoosh. Whoosh.

Another scrap of darkness, like a comet, swooped down from the flies. In less than a second, it had gone. But the aerial ballet had started.

Conchita was reaching the climax of her aria. A twinge of apprehension about the scream touched her consciousness. Suddenly she doubted if she could do it. It was so unladylike and she realized she'd left it too late to bring sufficient dramatic tension to the moment.

At precisely the same moment she became aware of the dark, darting bombardment. She froze, transfixed with horror. Her mouth opened to scream but somehow she managed to keep singing. She ducked, running from one side of the stage to the other, hysterical with fear. Her hands flew to her hair, tearing at the wig, convinced the creatures were in it. The orchestra struggled to keep up with her.

The bats, who lived in the darkness of the fly galleries and grid, had woken up and begun their nightly hunt for food. They flew through the cave set, swooping and darting with a swiftness that the eye could hardly follow.

The audience sat bolt upright. It was new, this was news. Conchita Sanatini was actually acting. She was distraught, the final scream coming from her lips with a mighty surge from the orchestra. She fled from the stage.

Later Conchita was found trembling and incoherent, curled up in a corner behind an off-stage rock. She was assisted back to her dressing-table, weeping. She feared no one would ever take her work seriously again after such a public spectacle.

'Bats, Bats!' she cried. 'You didn't chase out the bats! There were dozens of bats! Escamillo . . .'

He stretched in his basket and blinked. Bats? He hadn't seen any. But he supposed they lived high up in the rafters. Had she expected him to climb up into the flies, as if it were a forest? And get all those nasty cobwebs in his coat?

Elizabeth came straight round to the dressing-room, wrapped in furs. 'Poor darling,' she purred. 'I forgot to warn you about zee bats.'

'You sound all right,' trembled Conchita suspiciously. 'What's happened to your cold?'

'Suddenly recovered, darling. Lots of Vitamin C. I feel wonderful. I shall be ready to take over my role at the next performance.'

'You did this on purpose,' Conchita gulped.

'Budapest,' said Elizabeth.

Conchita wept into Escamillo's long ruff. He was wet in minutes. He felt sorry for her. He might even give up drawing blood for her sake.

He thought longingly of freedom, stretching himself to his full three and a half feet. No lynx, not even a tame lynx, should have to monitor theatres for a living. He closed his eyes and dreamed he was running wild back home in a North American forest, climbing high into the remoter regions, the wind streaming through his fur . . .

Conchita . . .
assisted back to her dressing-table, weeping. She feared no
one would ever take her work seriously again after such a

GLAD TIDINGS

Sky did not understand Christmas. Nor did he understand his name. He knew he wasn't blue, nor did he walk in the sky. It was as much a mystery to Sky as this intangible thing called Christmas.

It was coming, they said. He looked out of the window in case it turned the corner of the road. There was a feeling of excitement in the air; he could also sense tension, strain, pressure.

There was a lot to be done for Christmas, they said. He helped by digging up a few bulbs from the rock hard earth, and brought them indoors. Apparently this was not helpful and he was chased from the house.

One evening there was a lot of noise and a big box came down from the loft. He was not allowed up into the loft despite three lightning attempts to climb the ladder. He sniffed around the box. Was this dry, metallic smell Christmas?

Household activity zoomed to the speed of light as the box was opened. Sky found himself draped in silver tinsel, even his long bushy tail was entwined with the itchy stuff.

'Oh look, doesn't Sky look sweet? Shall we put him on top of the Christmas tree?'

Sky's ears twitched. He saw that they had brought some of the garden indoors now. Was Christmas then a tree? All this fuss for something that grew in the garden the year round? Perhaps he could help by climbing the Christmas tree and rearranging the tantalizing white angels that swung like clusters of butterflies. Everyone shrieked.

'Get that cat down from the tree!'

'He's trampling on my new Christmas paper!'

'That's a present, idiot. Get off!'

Sky was not sure what he had done that was wrong. Their voices were angry. It was all participation as far as he was concerned.

A fat dead white bird appeared in the kitchen, headless, with bent legs strung up. Sky investigated it with interest. It might smell better if it wasn't stone cold.

'No!' someone scolded. 'Sky, you naughty cat!' He was pulled off and shut in a different room. He slunk under a low bookcase, flattening himself into an impossible shape, his lemony eyes mere slits. Now he knew what Christmas was. Christmas was anger, shortage of time, frantic activity, irritability, loss of affection. Sky had not sat on a decent lap for nearly a week. He tucked his nose under his tail. Perhaps when he woke up it would be all over.

But the next day was even worse. He cowered behind

the pandemonium. His breakfast was late and his stomach clawed at itself. The house was invaded by strangers, new feet, new smells, loud hearty voices. Quite soon he had a headache.

The carpet disappeared under a mountain of crumpled paper and Sky got Sellotape stuck on his paws, then on his whiskers. A new woman took him aside and gently teased them off. She slipped him a piece of turkey from her plate. Was Christmas looking up? His spirits rose tentatively. He climbed the tree to see if anything else was looking up.

The crash shook the house. Shouts and shrieks deafened the television. He was put out, trembling with fright. Sky couldn't understand. He was allowed to climb trees outside.

The ground was covered in white wet stuff. He shook his paws fastidiously and shrank within his fur. He took shelter beneath a small bush, crouching under leaves that feathered him with cold white dust.

Light burst through the front door and they were all coming out, clad in scarves and woolly hats, clutching torches that swung like arc lamps. They set off, tramping down the road.

Sky followed at a distance, curious, afraid of being left behind. Perhaps they were so angry with him that they were never coming back.

They stood in a group outside a house. 'Away in a manger,' they began to sing.

'Awaaaaaaaaay,' Sky bawled.

'Shoo, cat. Go home . . .'

'Once in Royal David's City . . .'

'Royeweoall,' Sky joined in counter-tenor.

'Sshh, go away. Stop that awful racket.'

'He's only trying to sing with us,' said the new woman.

She picked him up and tucked him inside her anorak, despite his snowy wet fur. Sky dug his claws into her sweater, still growling and carolling.

They took him home and he slept on her lap while they watched television. Then the dead bird was dismantled for sandwiches and he got all sorts of juicy, delicious scraps. It was too far for the new woman to go home, so they made up a bed for her on the sofa. He curled on her feet, warm and sleepy and replete.

If this was Christmas, then he'd go for it, every time.

SCALLYWAGS

We are three rescued kittens, thrown out when only two-day-old scraps, barely alive. We knew nothing about it at the time, clinging to our mother with glued eyes. Now we live with our foster mother (human) and real mother, Sasha. The problem is that our rescuer is supposed to choose between us which she will keep. Two to stay, two to go.

We all love this woman dearly, in our different ways. Daisy is flighty and dotty, dances everywhere, never keeping still, and is either too busy playing to eat at all or else gobbles frantically in order to get back to some game. Caspian (or Paddington Bear as he is called in moments of hilarity) is a gorgeously handsome Long-haired Blue and lives on his looks. I truly love everyone and prove it with dedicated people watching, head nudging, power purring, hourly kisses. I also do a pretty good imitation of a fur scarf round broad shoulders.

We are, however, only here on approval.

We do try to help.

Yesterday we rearranged her flower arrangement. It was sitting in the fireplace which was a daft idea since even the thickest dumbhead knows that flowers don't grow in fireplaces.

She was not pleased. We strew it all over the carpet which gave the room a much more natural appearance. It looked like a garden. Dried flowers, ferns, grasses tossed in gay abandon. Then we jumped on her back and sat on her heels, dug our needle-like claws into her bare legs while she tried to clear up the mess. Such fun.

Today we were going to dismantle the central heating. This means fiddling with valves and things and pulling up the carpet. We got quite a bit of the carpet up before he discovered us and shut us in our pen. I ask you. We're far too big for that pen now and there's only a stupid Smartie box on a string to play with and a big stuffed white dog that's no good for anything except dragging around.

We set up a pitiful chorus of squeaks and she let us out. It always works. Caspian went and thanked her. He's so sweet-natured and well-behaved and polite, it's really sickening. He's also unfairly handsome, with a long, thick silvery-grey coat like velvet and big blue eyes.

'Oh what a dear little teddy-bear face,' everyone cries, cuddling him. He's so good-natured, he never bites back. He also washes everything in sight. Show him a bar of soap and he'd wash it.

Daisy, my baby sister, has the highest IQ. I'll give her that. Any problem that needs solving, she'll solve it. Set her

a puzzle like how to unravel several cotton reels simultaneously, and she'll work it out. She hides all our toys then
finds them again with ecstatic purrs, producing them like a
conjuror's trick. She's also called a Blue, though she's mostly
grey, short-haired and smooth, one pink paw and a sprink-
ling of silvery fur round her eyes like pearly eyeshadow,
smudged and ethereal.

I haven't got a proper name. I've been nameless for weeks.
I'm variously called Muffin-for-the-moment, Biscuit,
McVitie, Osbourne, Jasper and McGyver, because of my
pale honey coat. I am the colour of wholemeal flour, mango
flesh, an undercooked brandysnap, milky coffee, caramel, a
fresh mushroom, honeyed waffle, alabaster, a macaroon, a
crumpet, an oatcake. There are two long rust streaks down
my back, tinted with speckled gold and five little ones on
the top of my head. I am sprinkled gold with a light brown
necklace from a distant Pharaoh around my neck. She wants
to call me Sandy. I feel like an Oliver.

'You have such beautiful eyes,' she says, a little afraid of
me. 'Slanting like some ancient Egyptian statue, yet they
are as bright as amber traffic lights. I'm sure the great cat
goddess Bast looked just like you.'

I look at her remotely, mysteriously. It may be that I am
a descendant of Bast. My eyes are the same.

I'm the ringleader. I think of everything first. First born,
first out of the nest, first to eat from a grown-up saucer,
first up a tree, first to fall out of a tree, first under the
shed, first to use a flowerbed.

This morning was so beautiful I thought some indoor
gardening to be an ideal occupation. She has more plants
than she can cope with. I sat on several flower pots, pruned
the over-long and trailing ivy, chewed thoughtfully on a

begonia, discovered ants in the moneymaker and sent it flying immediately. Urgh! Surely she did not want ants on her windowsill? Unthinkable.

I was scolded (unfairly), but when she discovered the ants in the scattered earth on the floor, she changed her mind and covered me with hugs and kisses on the top of my head.

We moved on to outdoor gardening and helped plant out the seedling lettuces. We did not quite get the same straight rows she put out, but for a first time our efforts were pretty impressive. We made a lot of extra holes too ... everywhere. You never know when she might need them.

'Muffin-for-the-time-being, please get out of the way or you might get your tail chopped off.'

I am studying the edge cutter. The noise is fascinating and the way all the bits of grass go flying into the air. I also run behind the lawn mower, prancing, attacking, stalking. This worries everyone but I don't care. Wait till I find out how the car works.

When it's raining we help her with the filing. She is absolutely hopeless at it; no method at all. Piles lean all over the carpet and on her desk. The bookcases are stuffed with paper. We make an excellent job of the filing. You could call it a flying start. Now she can see everything ... all at once. We thought she would be pleased. She's always saying that no one gives her a hand. And we gave her twelve paws.

'Oh my goodness...' She was speechless. 'Muffin-for-the-moment, I know this is all your doing. Get off my desk. Go away. Sit down and behave.'

I have never sat down and behaved in my entire life. Nor has Crazy Daisy. We are either bouncing around like rubber balls or flaked out, totally horizontal. Isn't that a wasp, bee, fly? Gotcha! Whoops! Watch out, something's going over . . .

'Oh no, my clock. My precious French chiming clock. A wedding present. Muffin, what am I going to do with you?'

Give me a proper name, I hope. It's not much to ask.

I sniff the pieces curiously. Boring. Not worth all these wails and feminine tears. I help her again with picking up the pieces. The case is not broken but the inside is pretty shaken up. Who wants all that chiming anyway, not even in English. You'd think she would be grateful. She won't have to wind it up now.

'I'm not going to keep you,' she stormed. 'I'm sending you back. I'll keep Caspian, and his mother, Sasha. He's no trouble but you and Daisy are driving me round the bend.'

The words froze in the air though it was still morning and the sun dappled the room with freckles. Send us back? Back to where? Where did we come from? Me and little Daisy? My baby sister was prancing around, heedless, chasing a butterfly. She never listened to anything, as innocent as a rose petal. I couldn't tell her. She has to be protected.

I went into the garden, quite sedately for me. My legs were weak with disbelief. What did send us back mean? We had always been here. My earliest memory is of being crowded in a basket and being jolted along in the back of a van, very late at night. We crawled out on to the floor of a kitchen, three tiny, lost and helpless handfuls of fur. But I was also curious and began to sniff the new scents while the others climbed into a cocoon of flannelette and nuzzled against our mother.

'I can't believe that anyone would throw them out at two days old,' the woman was saying, stroking each of us carefully with one finger. 'It's so cruel.'

'I don't think they realized that a female cat could become pregnant at such a young age. She's only a kitten herself, barely nine months.'

We are a single-parent family, I thought sleepily against the silver fur of her stomach, with a teenage mum.

Today I'm into housework. This water stuff is fascinating. I am watching the drips falling from the tap, mesmerized, the water swishing round the bowl, the long sweep-sweep of the floor mop as it cuts a dark swathe over the lino.

'Out, out,' she cries, trying to catch us all as we attack the mop in commando waves. We are fantastic, sliding everywhere, patterning the wet lino with paw marks, causing havoc.

We are all water mad. We sit in the bathroom basin for this washing stuff. So sometimes we get our tails wet. She has to spit around us. We skate up and down the empty bath when she tries to clean it. Show us a dripping tap and we are hooked for the duration.

Sewing is also good for a laugh. Sitting on the sewing brings the whole operation to a standstill. Tipping over the sewing box is hilarious, though she seems to be worried about us stepping on pins and needles. Cutting out heralds a good old slide on the flattened material spread on the floor, boxing clever with the folds, rolling ourselves up into a pancake of fabric and sweet innocence. She laughs. She didn't really want to sew anyway.

The same as she doesn't really want to cook, but she has to. It's part of some arrangement that she does all the work. We help with the cooking, like walking across a hot stove, peering into the food mixer, transfixing the slowly revolving microwave with crossed-eyes.

'No, no,' she cries in desperation, trying to protect her

embryo meal from the marauders, removing kittens from every surface. 'I'm going mad.'

She rushes about, hauling us out of this and that, watching we don't get burned, chopped, frozen. 'It's no good. I'll have to shut you out.'

She bundles us out and shuts the door. We set up a pitiful squeak from the hall that says we are cold, lost, frightened, sorry, won't ever do it again, etc. After about a minute she lets us in. In one bound all three of us are back on the working-tops to see what she's doing. Wow, curry! Great! Cheesecake, great! Chocolate trifle, we'll try anything.

She often cries. It's very disturbing. We don't understand this crying business. I do my best with nudging her face with my wet nose and purring loudly in her ear. Caspian tries to distract her with his amazing good looks and sedate manner. Daisy dances about a lot, making herself extra tiny and amusing; she puts on a kind of cabaret show. It makes the woman stop crying, and then she cuddles us all in turn, including Sasha who is turning into a mother-groupie. I suppose it's because they have something in common.

It's obvious that they love each other. They have a kind of rapport.

Two to go and two to stay. It's getting near crunch time. She'll have to make up her mind soon. We're getting bigger.

'Muffin and Daisy will have to go,' she says, hugging us both. 'Sasha has had four homes already; it just wouldn't be fair to move her again. And Caspian is so beautiful, I couldn't bear to give him away. But I love you all. And what if I want to go? Who'd take on four cats? It would be totally over the top.'

Daisy and I did not know whether to be elated or

depressed. So, if in doubt, eat. We hunted about for edibles.
Raw potato? Biscuit wrapper? Cold tea bag?

Then we struck oil. I happened to be wandering along
this shelf of cookery books and knocked over a plastic container. The lid flew off and the contents spilled all over
the floor. The familiar scattering of hard little biscuits was
celestial music. We leapt on them as if Mafeking was round
the corner. It was her reserve stock of the non-addictive,
vitamin added, very expensive dried food she keeps for us.
And there were hundreds of them, everywhere. We went
galloping mad. It was party time . . .

The noise must have been like a herd of elephants breaking bamboo.

She heard. Who wouldn't?

'Oh my God, you'll all be sick,' she said, trying to scoop
up the dried food. After several minutes of fruitless scooping, she realized she was going about it in the wrong way.
We were scooped up instead, wildly protesting, twelve paws
wriggling, spines arching, necks elongating, and deposited
outside the door. Daisy, who has the speed of light, was
back in before the door closed.

'Oh no, you don't,' she said, blocking four pounds of
wriggling cat with eight and a half stone of determined
human. 'You've had quite enough. Look at your tummy.
Bloated.'

Daisy did a fast waddle towards the remaining morsels
but she did not stand a chance.

Nor did we. We disappeared to sleep off our unscheduled
midnight feast. We knew we had blown it. She would not
keep any of us now. She would exchange us all for one
well-behaved, house-trained, docile moggy with civilized
manners.

Every time she made a phone call, I jumped up beside her to monitor the call. Caspian kept guard on the car, casting his Cary Grant looks in her direction. Daisy . . . well, Daisy did her usual mad tail-chasing and leaping skywards to catch jets as they took off from Gatwick. I couldn't make her understand that this was serious stuff.

Sasha sat serenely in the garden, watching the antics of her uncontrollable offspring, giving the odd cuff if we came too near. Perhaps she knew something we didn't.

'I'm phoning about the rescued family,' I heard her saying on the phone later. 'It's not a case of deciding which kitten to keep, but of deciding which ones to send away. And I can't do that even though they are driving me mad. They are as naughty as can be. It's like having a house full of disobedient children. But there you are, I can't decide. Maybe I'll have to keep them all.'

The burden of dismissal rolled from my apprehensive mind. I sit in the washbasin, adoring her as I watch the dripping tap and this curious make-up ritual. I breathe the scent of her skin, dig my claws into her hair as I climb on to her shoulders and curl round her neck. I love the clearness of the water and the crystal droplets as she splashes her face; the two of us are bonded.

So that's how we all came to stay. I don't know what we did to make it happen since we are still an army of scallywags. The plants have all been removed. Ornaments packed away. Food hidden. Cupboard doors locked or blocked. The Christmas tree only lasted minutes. We took down the decorations as fast as she put them up. We haven't given up on reaching the hanging nut bags in the trees she puts out for the birds. We devour a way through any packaging that holds food. We are learning how to key the computer. We help with printing out, giving the pages an encouraging bash when she isn't watching.

She calls me Muffin now as well. Perhaps when I am grown up, I will get a new name. I still go for Oliver.

DING, DONG, BELL

Ding, dong, bell
Pussy's in the well.

They were chasing her, boys with loud voices and grubby worn trainers. They ran, helter-skelter, down the slippery, rough paved street, throwing cans and stones. A stone caught her sharply on the rump and she slithered to a halt momentarily, then leaped over a wall and fled along the top, her lithe black shape silhouetted against the night sky.

Danger was still in the air; she smelled the acrid whiff of evil. A hand caught her legs and pulled her off the wall. She struggled fiercely, biting and scratching, but the grip was strong and she was helpless. Her green eyes glinted as she looked at her captor, a skinny boy with a pimpled, pitted face like a doughnut.

He held her in a vice-like grip. She withdrew into herself, becoming a shape, knowing that her bones would snap like a bird's if he exerted any pressure.

Who put her in?
Little Johnny Green.

He hurried back to his friends and they gathered round, laughing and jeering. They tied a can to her tail. Tweaked her ears. Hung her upside down. She endured it all.

'C'mon, Johnny. Wotcha goin' to do wiv it?'

'Dunno. 'Ow about a nice swim?'

They took the grid off a drain and flung the cat into the sewer. They were doubled up with laughter, shoulders shaking, then ran off to find a new victim.

She spluttered as the murky water closed over her head. The air was fetid, stinking. She gasped for breath, vaguely aware that she was not alone. Rats scuttled by, wet and glistening, big, black slit eyes, mean and predatory.

There was a stream of garbage being carried along in the sluggish flow and her claws sank into a polystyrene fast-food container. It gave her just enough leverage to stop her sinking again.

Her small pink mouth opened in panic, hating the taste of the clogging viscous liquid that filled her lungs. Her stomach rolled in agony. She could not even bring it up in her unnatural position.

She clung to the hamburger box for several minutes, swirling round, till a sudden input surge from an office building sent it bobbing out of her grasp. With a leap of desperation, she clawed herself on to a narrow ledge that ran above the level of the water.

When the retching was spent, she cautiously and fastidiously moved away, further along the ledge. Black creatures like snakes swam below her; more rats scuttled along the ledge, confident of their superiority.

It was impossible to open her glued-up eyes. She let them stay closed, weariness coming over her in jaded waves, passed fighting the inevitable, not caring much whether she lived or died in the darkness. She had scavenged the streets for long enough, finding food in dustbins and gutters, catching mice on derelict ground, fawning around building sites for unwanted scraps. She remembered being with a human. She remembered a woman with a quiet voice and trembly knobbly hands trying to open a tin. One day the woman vanished and the cat forgot her own name.

She gnawed at the string tied on her tail. It took time but eventually the tin can fell with a plop into the water.

The level of the water was going down and the heat of the place dried her fur into spiky points. She lay still, wondering what she should do and how to get out.

Noises rang continuously in tinny echoes along the tunnels; and always the water rushing by, sibilant and slapping, the undulating waves like some primeval monster rising from the deep.

Eventually the nausea settled and her stomach rumbled with hunger. This was nothing new. The smell of rats was overwhelming but she could not work out how she could catch one without entering the black water again. She crawled along the narrow edge, ears alert, her senses taking in clues. This patch was dry, this cold; this wall had water running down it. She lapped at a puddle of rain before it fell into the flow and the moisture cleared her clogged throat. She sniffed around carefully to remember the place. Rainwater meant survival. She did not want to be swept along with the other debris to wherever it went.

Her whiskers twitched, swooping forward with a tremor of new awareness. Different rat smell. Small, dry, helpless. She pounced on the nest, dragging a baby rat out, and ran back along the ledge with it hanging from her mouth like a string of liquorice.

She crunched in panic, letting the head and tail fall away, afraid the mother might return at any moment. Nothing happened. Hunger fuelled her courage and she crept back, neatly extracting another from the nest with a deft paw. She retreated a long way back into the tunnel before she ate it. The second tasted better. It tasted of hope.

Her recurring dream was of a whirlpool. Deep, black, swirling water that devoured everything with crab-like claws reaching out. She knew that the time would come when she would be swallowed by the water. How could she stay there for ever? There was no way out. One day the level of the water would rise above the ledge and she would be sucked under. Her last breath would be fetid, her last thought of those endless bright stars that she no longer saw.

Who pulled her out?
Little Tommy Stout.

The bells went down for the third time that night. Blue Watch rolled out of their bunks and in thirty-three seconds flat were riding the pump as they struggled into their uniforms and helmets.

'The third shout, I ask you,' Tom groaned, climbing into his boots and leggings. The storm had raged over the city all night. They had been called out to two blocks of flooded basement flats and had been pumping for hours. This was a burst water main, escaping down to the main sewer level. The sewers were of Victorian construction and the extra volume of water would put a strain on the already crumbling interior tunnels.

'Get a crew down there,' said the station officer briskly. 'Tom and Arthur. Check what's happening. Someone reported a noise.'

Big deal, thought Tom, fumbling with the fastenings of his tunic. He stared at the yellow street lights as they wavered in the streaming rain like fireworks about to go out.

'Who's a midget, then?' a mate jeered.

'Mega-gnome,' grinned another.

Tom dredged up a smile. He was sick of their taunts. He was tired of being the shortest man on Blue Watch. Where could he get growth hormones? He longed to be tall. Why was he always the one they stuffed through pantry windows, shoved down coal shutes, heaved through lift traps?

But did he ever get to rescue a damsel in distress? Never. He was usually mown down in the rush of the big fellas to the bedroom door.

The water main was spewing upwards like an Icelandic geyser, tossing hundreds of gallons of water into the air. An oily river slick threatened the roadway, sweeping away traffic cones, dustbins, rocking cars on submerged wheels.

'Numbers one, three and five pumps,' the station officer ordered.

Tom strapped on his compressed air set. He'd been down a sewer before. It was no picnic.

'Sprout. Lestor.'

'Guv!'

'Down you both go.'

'Guv!'

Tom lifted the heavy manhole cover and felt for the first rung of the iron ladder. He adjusted the mouthpiece of the oxygen, took a deep breath and descended.

God, it was awful. The darkness and the smell. His flashlamp caught the eyes of a rat in its beam and Tom shuddered. He hated rats. He knew the layout of the main sewer; it was the tributaries that would confuse him. He hitched a guideline to a rung and let it run out behind him. The sooner this was done, the better. The water was lapping over the top of his waders, running down into his boots, squelching around his socks.

His stomach heaved.

'Hell's bells,' gulped Lestor.

A black shape hurled itself at Tom, sending him staggering. Claws dug into the front of his neck despite the heavy collar and breathing apparatus. He prised the creature off and it fled into the darkness. The flashlamp caught a glimpse of long black tail on a ledge. Dammit, a cat.

Tom eventually found where some wall masonry had crumbled. It did not look like a major fall. He made sure. He could return now. He turned to go back, feeling for the guideline in the darkness, hating every step he took through the stinking flow.

He felt around his belt for the line. His fingers found nothing. It had gone. This was trouble and he would be in bad trouble. He had broken the first rule of a fireman. Make sure the guideline is secure. He hadn't checked.

'Lestor?'

There was no answer.

He looked at his air gauge. He had thirty-five bars, about fifteen minutes of oxygen left. No need to panic, he told himself, trying to remember the route he had taken. It couldn't be far. Go against the tide of water.

Hostile green eyes glared at him, glinting, a low rumbling growl coming from its throat. Tom was momentarily caught in admiration. The cat was stuck down this pit of horror yet still had the courage to defend its territory. It did not occur to him that the cat might be wild. Tom went towards it, hand outstretched.

'Puss, puss,' he hissed through the respirator, a weird sound.

The cat paused. She had not heard a human voice for many days. It threw her but she did not trust this lumbering figure.

'Come on, old thing. Let's get you out of here.'

The cat crouched back on the narrow ledge, snarling, ready to spring into flight.

'Fish and chips,' said Tom. 'Like some nice fish and chips, mate?'

The words were soothing and familiar. The woman had said that, often. She went out somewhere and came back with this delicious food in a greasy bag that she shared with the cat.

Tom sensed that the cat had relaxed its guard momentarily. He moved as fast as a cat himself, snatching the animal off the ledge, pulling it against his chest. The cat hung, remembering another vice-like grip. But this time no one tweaked her ears or tied a can to her tail.

Tom stuffed the cat inside his tunic and winced as sharp claws dug through his tee-shirt, drawing blood.

'Right,' he said, swallowing the pain. 'Let's get you and me out of this damned place.'

He retraced his steps, remembering now with uncanny accuracy the vagaries of the tunnels. He came to the iron rungs of the ladder and saw his guideline tangled in it like limp string. He climbed up and out into the fresh night air, pulling off his respirator. Tom felt taller, grinned. The air smelt like spring without a crocus or daffodil in sight.

'Where you been, man?' said Lestor.

> What a naughty boy was that
> To try to drown poor pussy cat,

Johnny Green stared at his precious collection of football cards. They were sodden, colours running, swirling in a muddy mess. The basement flat was flooded. His father was yelling at him. Johnny took no notice, deaf with despair. He could never replace his collection. It guaranteed his leadership of the gang. He had nothing left.

> Who never did him any harm
> And killed the mice in his father's barn.

'We'll get rats after this,' said his father, pulling up a soaking carpet. 'You wait and see. Pity we haven't got Gran's cat. She was a great mouser.'

Tom stretched out in the mess room. He'd showered, got the stink off, changed. The mug of strong sweet tea in his hand was the best brew in the world. He poured out a saucer of milk and put it on the floor.

'Here, Blackie. Drink up. This is your home now.'

The cat tensed, trembling, remembering her name at last.

KIPPERBANG'S
NEW PET

Kipperbang had spent all of the previous summer searching for a pet of his very own. Humans had pets, so why shouldn't a cat, especially a small angelic-looking tortoiseshell with solemn green eyes. His thought processes were relatively similar to humans', but a lot less confused. He called food food, and sleep sleep and in and out meant exactly that.

He never fudged issues. Humans had different meals at different times, sleeping habits were notoriously unreliable and Kipperbang could not make head nor tail of their goings in or out.

But having pets he did understand. He had wanted one of his own ever since he realized that his mistress adored her pet. She was always talking about it to her friends.

First Kipperbang found a nice round stone for a pet but it became pretty boring and didn't play much. Then he grew very fond of a large paper bag until his mistress rode over it on her bicycle and threw it away. His favourite had been the ladybird, whom he named Ruby. He kept her for days in the greenhouse till one day she flew home because her house was on fire and her children were all alone.

Kipperbang did understand that it was an emergency but still he moped for days.

He discovered his next pet rolling around the garden. It rolled far more than the pebble ever did, and didn't tease him and fly off into the air and out of reach like the paper bag. He felt sure it wouldn't have any children, which was reassuring. It was completely the wrong shape for having children.

He picked it up carefully in his jaws, in case it got hurt. The ladybird had been particularly fragile and ferrying her around on his front paw had been very tiring.

He stopped in his tracks, alerted by something totally unexpected. This new pet had a taste, a delicious taste. Before he could stop himself, his jaws crunched on the taste, half closing. He jumped into the air, horror-stricken at what he had done, and sniffed cautiously. But no, it wasn't dead like some stupid, frittery bird or a petrified mouse. It didn't seem at all hurt apart from the holes punctured by his sharp teeth. It was already rolling merrily down the path.

Kipperbang was delighted. He had found an indestructible pet, childless, fun and a delicious taste. Who could ask for more? He bounced after it, his tail streaming in the wind.

'Look at Kipperbang,' said his mistress from the window. 'He's having such fun chasing something in the garden.'

He also discovered that he did not have to feed this pet, unlike the pebble and the paper bag, both of which had suffered from malnutrition but totally ignored his offerings of dead worms and squashed spiders. Even the ladybird had found all her own greenfly in the greenhouse and turned up her sweet nose at his little treats.

'Kipperbang is so happy these days,' his mistress said to the other human who lived in the house, a giant with large feet and a booming voice that offended Kipperbang's delicate hearing. 'He always looked so lonely.'

'Don't be daft, lass. How could a cat be lonely?'

'He used to sit for hours on the rockery, just staring at the view.'

'That's what cats do. They contemplate life.'

'I don't think it's quite as simple as that,' she said.

It was a wonderful summer for Kipperbang. His new pet was so undemanding. It never got jealous if Kipperbang was suddenly distracted by a bird or an ants' nest or encouraging a frog into leaps along a flowerbed. It never got annoyed if left out in the rain or abandoned behind the garden shed. Kipperbang had never known such a tolerant nature. It was the perfect pet.

Kipperbang sauntered into the kitchen one day, the usual contented expression on his face, both luminous green eyes glowing with happiness. It was suppertime and he smelled his favourite coley in the air; visions of the succulent white flakes and tasty juice made his mouth water.

But he sensed immediately that his mistress's mind was not on his supper. She was standing close to the giant and there was wet on her cheeks.

'Six months? Oh darling, I shall miss you so much. Do you really have to go?'

'Six months will soon pass.' Kipperbang flinched at the booming voice.

'But what shall I do without you, pet?'

'You'll be all right. Just so long as you don't find someone else,' he growled.

Kipperbang curled himself round her ankles. He hoped she'd find someone else less noisy, with smaller feet and a better sense of direction. He nosed her ankle, sniffing her skin, leaving the oil from his fur to mark his territory and convey his concern and sympathy.

'I shall be so lonely without you, pet,' she went on, more wet appearing on her cheeks. Kipperbang watched it trickle down her face, fascinated. Where had it come from? Was she making it herself? How incredibly clever. He gazed up at her in admiration as a drop fell on his head and made him jump.

It jerked him into activity. He raced into the garden. Of course she would be lonely without her pet. This he understood completely. He felt a glow of love and gratitude for the way she fed and loved him and tickled him in all the right places. It was the very least he could do. He would share his pet with her.

He ran to where he had left his pet sunbathing among the marigolds. It was waiting patiently, a few marigold petals stuck to its inside like confetti. Kipperbang took it up gently, savouring the strong taste.

He took his pet indoors, proudly, and laid it with reverence at his mistress's feet. He stepped back, confident of their mutual adoration of his pet.

She bent down and picked it up. 'Urgh! Kipperbang, what have you brought in? What a dirty old yogurt pot. It's absolutely revolting.'

She rushed over to the sink and Kipperbang watched with horror as she drowned his pet in a stream of water. She shook off the drips and threw the pot into a carrier bag hanging behind the door.

'Another one for the play school,' she said, wiping her hands.

Kipperbang could not touch his supper. He pushed the fish around politely; it tasted like cardboard, the juice like vinegar. He pretended to clean his whiskers.

He waited patiently till they took their supper into the other room. He jumped on to the draining board, stepped over the mugs and peered into the carrier bag.

The sight that met his eyes made his fur stand on end. There were dozens of pots bundled up together, all different shapes and sizes. He was astonished. Where had all those children come from? And in such a short time? He tried to find his pet but it was impossible.

He wandered disconsolately out into the garden and climbed on to the rockery. He sat staring at the gloom as the evening light faded and the moon rose like a hunter in the sky.

'I can't think what's the matter with Kipperbang,' his mistress said from the window. 'He hasn't moved for hours.'

Kipperbang sat as still as an Indian chief and as stony-faced. Not a muscle moved. No one knew that his heart was slowly breaking. Now he would have to find yet another pet.

THE ROWAN TREE

The rowan had been growing on the chalky slopes of Chantonbury Hill for several decades. It was not particularly beautiful, barely twenty feet high, and its yellow-grey trunk had longitudinal cracks. Its branches were spindly, pinnate leaves toothed, long fingers of twigs craving air and space in the dense woodland that skirted the rounded hillock above.

Mishka knew the rowan well. He had sharpened his claws on it many times. Its bark suited the sensitive nerve ends that were housed in the sheath of skin encompassing the nails and could send exquisite sensations along his limbs. He liked the scent of the slim and downy buds in spring and the bridal flowering in May.

Mishka lived in a humped cottage that huddled in

the dip of the Weald below Chantonbury Hill, once a labourer's cottage, now the home of a couple who owned a restaurant in Worthing. The third floor was only an attic with a single postage stamp window like an eye on the world; the several roofs sloped with the weight of time and years; the crooked chimney had not seen a fire for half a century.

He lived well-fed but unloved. They were both far too busy. He ate restaurant food, brought home in cat-bags; they made sure he had the necessary feline vaccination jabs; he never slept on a lap. He spent his long days and nights roaming the South Downs in search of a voice. They didn't speak to him. They spoke over him.

'Have you fed the cat?'

'We'd better put the cat out.'

He brought them gifts in vain. Leaves, twigs, bark, sheep's fleece, a stone from the top of the hill. They did not notice. It was the stone that caused all the trouble. The escalation of events flowed from that one small stone, rolling and gathering an electromagnetic force, orbiting electrons to a central nucleus.

Chantonbury Hill had long been the source of strange rumours. Its history went back to before memory. There had been an Iron Age fort on the hill four hundred years before Christ. That was so long ago; the souls of those people were lost in a cold mist of brutality and hardship. The Romans had fought with a garrison on the high point and built a temple. In 1760 the eccentric Charles Goring, then still a boy living at nearby Wiston Park, planted a circle of beech trees on the crest of the South Downs to clothe the wild, wind-blown top with a crown of green and gold. It could be seen for miles. It became the best known summit in Sussex.

These were the known facts of Chantonbury Hill. There were other more sinister tales – stories of nightly rituals, of black worship, of the appearance of the devil. Few went on the hill after dark. Only the mentally reckless ran round it seven times going backwards at midnight. Sometimes people saw a blue ball of light hovering in the trees. They said it was the devil bringing a bowl of soup or a cup of milk to the revellers.

Mishka was put out far more often than he was called in. He felt that being ignored and rejected so often had crippled his spirit. Yet he did his best to become accepted as part of the household: he purred enthusiastically in praise of restaurant left-overs; he jumped on laps; he rubbed ankles. All to no avail. They were not cat people.

'Have you fed the cat?'

'Put that cat out and come to bed.'

'Both matters are of sublime indifference to me.'

So Mishka roamed the Weald, travelling miles, watching, listening, recording scents and habits. He had an academic knowledge of the area. He knew, for instance, that the rowan was moving. It was climbing the hill.

At first, Mishka thought his memory was playing tricks, that his perception of the location was at fault. He marked the territory with precision. It puzzled him. He could not be wrong five days in a row.

He curled up in a tangle of spent growth a short distance from the tree and settled down to wait. He had infinite patience. The light faded and his stomach rumbled. He thought with longing of halibut and plaice from the plates of the restaurant, grilled kidneys and crab terrine. The saliva dribbled from his mouth but he kept his green eyes on the rowan, curious but a little afraid.

Dark clouds hid the pale face of the moon and a low wind moaned through the wooded hillside. Leaves rustled in whispered talk and the scampering of tiny feet alerted Mishka to the living night world. He blinked and yawned.

A long root appeared through the earth, seeking substance, moving like a thin brown worm. It clawed its way up the slope and took hold of a sapling which cowered under the tension. A sound of tearing grew as the rowan hauled itself out of the earth and climbed a few feet up the hillside, earth and stones cascading noisily, the soul of the timber groaning at the effort.

Mishka stared, transfixed. The rowan had moved. He had never seen a tree move before. The old root crater slowly filled, the way sand would dribble into a pit dug by a child, and in a few minutes there was nothing to be seen of the discarded hole.

Suddenly the rowan seemed to become aware that it was being watched and its branches swept the ground like tentacles, sucking at the earth for scents. Miskha fled. Moving trees were highly unnerving. He scuttled through the leaves, down the steep path, and took the fields to the cottage.

'It's after midnight,' he heard someone say. 'I've a good mind to let that cat stay out all night.' Mishka put on a turn of speed and shot between the legs that stood in the doorway.

'Covered in muck and leaves as usual,' the other complained.

He cleaned himself up as best he could. He was still

trembling from his fright. He would have to be careful if he was going to watch the rowan again.

By mid October the rowan was hung with clusters of bright red berries and it stood almost at the top of the hill. Mishka was sick with worry. Something was desperately wrong. He could feel it in the air. The rowan had changed shape, becoming darker, taller, thinner, with branches that waved like arms, twigs becoming long fingers. The cat no longer sharpened his claws on the yellowy bark, wary of some reaction. He swore he could hear the tree breathing.

Despite his dread, he was fascinated. His damned curiosity superseded his good sense and he was drawn again and again, in any weather, to the top of Chantonbury Hill where the circle of proud beeches stood in all their autumnal glory.

It was an odd day, a Thursday that felt different. Nothing seemed to be stirring, as if the pall of silence and stillness heralded something ominous. Mishka saw a smooth whitish stone he liked very much and patted it about. When he decided to return home for his supper, he took it carefully in his mouth as a gift. A sudden hissing among the leaves alarmed him and he dropped the stone. It slithered down the slippery slope like a living thing.

It seemed to be a signal. Positively ionized air molecules charged the atmosphere.

An observer from miles away said he saw a light in the sky right over the landmark of beeches.

Mishka never remembered having that supper because by the time he reached the cottage the loose windows were rattling, doors banging, the chimney howled, and outside branches were beginning to snap. The wind gathered in the sky, devils flew, wisps of witches clung desperately to their whirling garments.

The hill opened its jaws and out rushed a terrifying hurricane. Senses quickened to danger and the small animals scampered to their lairs. The wind roared across the country, gathering trees and tiles and fences and hedges in its path. Gusts of ninety-five miles per hour ripped down electricity cables, telephone wires, road signs.

The hurricane caught the rowan in its vortex and spun it round, wrenching its heart out as the wind flung it into the air. The tree shrieked as it was rent asunder and its roots torn from the earth. It split lengthways like straw and the essence of the tree coiled itself into a long wraith and reached out to the blackened sky. It freed itself from the dying tree and raced away from the evil centre of the storm, shooting upwards, starwards and beyond the holocaust.

Mishka cowered among the flying debris, fur and whiskers flattened, eyes wide with horror as he watched the play of quivering lights. The beeches toppled, one by one, with shrieks and groans of cracking wood that made the earth shudder. Mishka was sure that the devil was let loose from a bondage, wreaking vengeance on the whole of the South of England. This mighty wind cut swathes through forests and woodlands, uprooted thousands upon thousands of trees, flung cars in the air, ripped off roofs, toppled chimneys, stirred the seas into a fury.

By morning the storm was petering out; little runs of wind played among the devastated landscape in an apologetic way. Nothing looked the same. The crest of beeches had gone. Mishka could not believe his eyes. Giant trees lay toppled and helpless, great mounds of roots exposed to the empty sky. Dead animals lay under fallen branches. He limped home.

A hundred-year-old oak lay half across the roof of the cottage like a long arm. They were packing the car with belongings.

'I'm not staying here another night. I never wanted to live in the country in the first place. Now we've no roof.'

'Have you see the cat?'

'Damn the cat. Let's get to a hotel.'

'We'll let the cottage. I shan't want to live here again.'

Mishka watched them drive away. They never looked back. They never looked for him. He climbed in through a broken window and found some bread to chew. Then he discovered that the catch on the refrigerator door was not properly closed and a plate of cold salmon lasted him several days. Even raw bacon was acceptable. The buzz of log saws and the crackle of smoking bonfires filled the air of the last week of autumn.

Footsteps arrived at the cottage, light, quick, friendly.

'Of course, there's still a lot of repair work to be done. The roof has only been roughly patched.'

'I don't mind. I shall be here all day, working.'

Mishka found himself being picked up and inspected.

'Well, isn't he beautiful,' said the young woman. 'Does he go with the cottage?'

'They did say something . . . er . . . about a cat.'

'I'll keep him. I love cats.'

He found himself looking into bright black eyes and above them straight black brows. His whiskers quivered. She was young. She was lovely.

Her fingers found the engraved name tag around his neck, buried in his dense black fur. 'Mishka,' she read softly.

'Mishka, my Mishka. You are the perfect witch's cat,' she purred.

'I have so much to do,' she went on. 'I have this cottage to paint and the garden to plant. Pictures to draw and poems to write. And I love walking in the countryside. You'll come with me and be my guide, won't you? I bet you know every inch.'

Mishka overflowed with contentment. He nudged her pale ear, clawed at her long yellowy hair, caught the familiar scent of white flowerets.

'We shall be so happy together,' she whispered. 'But you know that already, don't you? Do you remember my name, Mishka? It's Rowan.'

CAT OF LA MANCHA

Donny stood in the doorway, drinking in the ice cool air with relief. He stood boldly, swishing his long sandy tail, breathing freedom. He had been imprisoned all night, pacing its mean confines, hunched by the cooling boiler, hating the sound of the great door slamming shut and the retreating footsteps of his jailor.

Night was a bad time. Every night shrank into solitary confinement. What assurance did he have that he would be let out in the morning, if ever? Supposing he was forgotten? No one said. No one spoke as they left him, not even a cheery goodnight. The door clanged and his prison was plunged into darkness.

But now it was morning and he was pushed out for exercise. The sense of freedom exploded in his head. He was reborn a knight, righting wrongs, putting the world to order.

He listened carefully, his eyes burning with the fire of inner vision. He might be old but he was still strong and bony, the adventures or misadventures of his past vivid in his mind. He was incensed by the injustices of the world, man to man, man to cat, cat to cat. He vowed that his last days would be spent as a Knight Errant. He would no longer be skinny, long-nosed Donny, Oriental Spotted Shorthair of sorts of 23 Arcacia Avenue, London W1, but Don Quixote of La Mancha, dauntless knight, idealist, visionary.

With this resolution strong in his heart, Don Quixote set forth on his travels. It was a pity he did not have a faithful squire. He would have liked the comfort and support of a companion, someone to help him up when he was knocked down. But there was no one he could call squire. He would have to do without and fight his battles alone.

With the frost puffing out his coarse spotted and splotched fur, Don Quixote sought his destiny, big paws paddling the cold earth without a single flinch. He could withstand pain. He wished he had a banner to fly, or a gauntlet to throw down, a sword or a lance: but he had only his claws and teeth as sharp as daggers.

Arcacia Avenue was a faded, blowsy street, slowly going down on its luck. The once gracious houses with columned porches were mostly converted into self-contained flats, discreet finance offices or dental surgeries. Cars were parked roadside all day. Council skips were stationed at either end of the road for the debris of renovations and conversions.

Suddenly Don Quixote's lynx-eyes caught sight of a monstrous giant of infamous and terrifying repute. It glowed red in the morning light, its huge mouth gaping and toothless. It would devour anything that came within biting distance.

The cat crouched low, girding his strength, long tail flicking with slowly growing anger. This monster had terrorized the street for long enough. He must be confronted. A low growl announced his intention, challenging the monster to fight. Don Quixote made a huge leap on to the smooth head, ready to sink his claws into the vulnerable tissue. But he clawed helplessly at the paintwork and slid off, landing in a heap on the grass verge.

'Silly cat,' said a girl, passing by. 'Whatever were you trying to do? It's only a letterbox, you know.'

But Don Quixote knew it was really a monster who had changed himself into a letterbox at the last moment. Monsters could do that. Don Quixote picked up his dignity, wishing he had armour and a helmet. How else would the girl know that he was a Knight Errant?

The girl posted a letter into the monster's mouth. She'd never see that again. 'You're a nice pussy,' she said. 'Where do you live?'

He tried to tell her that he lived in a prison. That the only people he knew were jailors, that there was an emptiness in his heart every time he heard the door clang shut.

'Who looks after you?'

He squirmed round her ankles, feeling their narrowness and smooth skin. Could a girl be his squire? It was a bit unusual but she was picking bits off his coat and stroking down his fur. All squirish activities. He was pondering this when he saw the stray, crawling along the rim of the skip, sniffing at a bag of refuse.

His lady . . . it was . . . it was his lady! A beauteous creature, thin and delicate, refined of feature, silver fur fanning her face like a halo of moonlight that made her aquamarine eyes glow with fervour. Her limbs stretched with an elegance that astonished him. She moved with the grace of a dancer, but she was so thin. Her bones would break if she fell. He wanted to protect her, fight dragons and ogres on her behalf. He would even fight the Great Destroyer.

Don Quixote ran to the stray, tail curved upwards, ready to greet her with courtesy, but she would have none of it. She hissed and spat, showing her sharp teeth. He wanted to tell her that she had nothing to be afraid of, that he would not hurt her.

'You leave that dirty cat alone,' said the girl. 'She's probably got fleas.'

He was appalled. The girl did not understand. The stray was a beautiful lady, simply living in the wrong environment. She should be sleeping on a silken cushion, fed morsels of chicken and cream.

Don Quixote backed away, reluctantly. There were so many things to do first. The air reeked of warlocks and wizards, vast armies to challenge in brave, unequal combat. Giants to topple, besieged citizens to rescue, bewitched kings to be set free. The world was a mass of unrighted wrongs. And he had so little time.

Then there was the most ferocious enemy of all – the Great Destroyer. Just the thought of it could make Don Quixote's blood chill, his fur stand on end with fear ... the heat of the beast's eyes, the way the earth was shorn, the roar of its terrible voice. The Great Destroyer would come soon, terrorizing the neighbourhood. No one was safe. To slay the Great Destroyer would be the culmination of his quest. Even his lady could not fail to admire him. He would dedicate his conquest to her.

He rubbed the girl's ankles again, trying to persuade her

to think kindly of the stray, to take her in perhaps, feed her, teach her the ways of a lady. He longed for a token to carry into battle.

The girl straightened up, dropping a tissue from her sleeve. Don Quixote pounced on it in triumph and carried it off. It was his token. He would lay it at his lady's feet when the Great Destroyer was slain.

'You're mad,' the girl laughed. 'What do you think you are doing? Cleaning up the street?'

Don Quixote drew himself up to his full size. He was magnificent and imposing, grey whiskers twitching with indignation. He might be old but he was no fool.

'Come and have some milk,' she went on. 'They're all out. I've got the place to myself.'

He followed her cautiously, swaying so that she would not notice the stray following some yards behind. He knew the stray was curious, hunger making her bold.

The place was an inn. He could not believe his eyes. The girl lived in an inn. There were old chairs and mattresses everywhere. He was actually looking for a castle, but an inn would do splendidly. It became a castle in his mind.

'We're not supposed to be here,' said the girl. 'We're squatters. They are going to do the place up, meanwhile it's somewhere out of the cold. The others go out most of the day, but I have a job in the evening, waiting on tables.'

Don Quixote sniffed around. He liked it. His own prison was bleak and cheerless, clinically tidy; this seemed a friendly, homely place with belongings strewn around in confusion, like Christmas morning.

She gave him some milk out of a bottle. The tin foil tray moved across the floor as he lapped. It smelled Indian. Different, he thought, Indian milk . . . and from a dish of silver. He stepped aside so that his lady could also drink, but in her unmannered haste she sent it flying.

'Oh dear,' said the girl, mopping it up with a cloth. 'That stray has got in. Shoo . . . shoo . . .'

Don Quixote rushed to his beloved's side as the stray cowered against a wall. How would he ever be dubbed a knight if he allowed his lady to be treated so unkindly? He nearly turned on the girl but remembered in time that she was also his squire. It was all so confusing. If only the girl could see that the little grey cat was really a lady.

'My goodness, you are a thin thing. I can see your bones sticking out . . . here, pussy, don't be afraid . . .'

Don Quixote saw that the girl held a moonbeam in her hand as the tin-opener pierced a tin of sardines and the tiny silver fish slithered on to a dish. His lady darted forward, her eyes gleaming, and she ate with exquisite cunning, fast and silently. He glowed in her satisfaction. He did not know how to thank his squire. What could he do for her? Did she have a giant she wanted killed? An ogre put to death? A king under enchantment? He would do anything for her.

The castle was warm and his lady fell asleep almost immediately on a heap of blankets. Her fur sparkled in the light from the fire and her ribs rose in a peaceful rhythm. Don Quixote was dizzy with happiness. A strange lump came into his throat and he swallowed awkwardly.

'I think there's a mouse in this cupboard,' said the girl. 'It's gnawed at some books.'

A mouse. It was almost beneath his contempt. To be asked to catch a mouse when he fought giants and monsters and could put to rout whole armies. How ridiculous. But he would do it for her. He dealt with the mouse with one accurate swipe. It fell, limp, lifeless. His squire was pleased.

She put the mouse in a bin and patted the cat's head several times.

'Clever old sausage,' she said. 'What else can I find for you to do?'

Don Quixote glowed in her admiration. Was that pat a dubbing? Could he count it as a dubbing? Knight of the Clever Old Sausage? Not exactly the title he would have liked. Knights always got a new name, but this . . . he would have preferred knight of the Amazing Bravery, or Knight of the Fiercesome Eye.

He froze suddenly. His sharp ears had picked up a distant noise and his blood nearly turned to water. He knew that sound, that terrible rumbling. The Great Destroyer was on its way to Arcacia Avenue. He jumped up on to a window-ledge and peered out into the street. The noise was growing louder, a cloud of dust on the horizon. He began to tremble. His moment had arrived. Now he would show his lady how brave he was; how he would lay down his life for her.

He ran out into the street, wishing he had a sword, a lance, shining armour. But he had nothing, only courage and a heart of gold.

The Great Destroyer stood at the end of the street, its hideous feet pawing at the grass verge. Obnoxious fumes spouted from its mouth. It faced Don Quixote with a roar that shook the paving stones.

Everyone backed out of the way. People rushed to move dustbins, bin bags, old bikes. Then they went indoors and closed their windows.

Don Quixote stood outside number 23, ears flattened, a low growl rumbling in his throat. He crouched flat to attack, but was suddenly blinded by a flashing light. He leaped back, unhurt but bewildered. Again he ran to attack but the

Great Destroyer repelled him with a blinding flash. Don Quixote reeled from the impact, lurching, falling. He staggered to his feet, bright lights stabbing his retina, unfocused, the world gone crazy. His fury sent him crashing into the Great Destroyer as it roared along the street.

'Get that cat out of my way,' the driver cursed.

The girl ran from the castle and cradled Don Quixote in her arms. He opened his eyes weakly and saw the face of his faithful squire.

'You foolish old thing,' she wept. 'Whatever did you think you were doing? That's the municipal lawn mower, doing the verges, and now on its way to the park. Did you think you could stop it?'

She carried him indoors and lay him on a blanket. Through a haze he saw his lady, now sitting up and grooming her silvery fur. Did she know how he had fought on her behalf? Was she proud of his exploits?

'You've given your head a right bump,' said the girl. 'But I don't think there's anything broken. Just you count yourself lucky, silly old thing.'

The world of reality was creeping slowly back and he saw things as they really were. His squire was changing to go and wait on tables. Some of the other squatters were returning. He and his lady were chased out into the street. She turned her back on him and began to follow the girl to the restaurant.

Don Quixote wandered back to number 23, head aching, and waited for his jailors to let him in. Another night in prison. Another night of solitary confinement. How could they do this to him?

'Donny, Donny, Donny,' the woman called.

She opened the door a crack, ungenerous even with light.

He slipped in, his lady's token between his teeth.

'Urgh! Look what that cat's brought in. A dirty bit of tissue.'

He stood boldly in the doorway, facing his jailors with courage. He would not be cowed. His mission in life was to right all wrongs. Could they not see he was Don Quixote, Cat of La Mancha, Knight Extraordinaire? Nothing could daunt his spirit.

MAFIA MOG

Mafia Mog was an enormous cat. He had the girth of a sumo wrestler. His long face fur and whiskers gave him a drooping mandarin moustache and beard. He was a deeply striped russet brown on fawn all along his body and down his tail. He had the low-slung walk of a lion.

He was also trouble. The neighbours closed their windows and shut their doors if they saw him coming. Car doors were locked, milk brought in, newspapers and mail retrieved quickly.

Nothing was beyond the reach of his claws in Mog's lumbering trail of mayhem.

They set up a residents' group, a kind of neighbourhood watch, to protect their homes from Mog's attentions. It was called GRMA, short for the Getting Rid of Mog

Association. The trouble was that they liked Felicia, the sweet, fair-haired young librarian who owned the cat. She had rescued him and brought him home from an animal sanctuary, a tiny honey-coloured bundle of fluff with pet-alled paws who grew and grew and grew.

'Your cat really is the limit,' said Felicia's immediate neighbour, coming out to collect what remained of her washing. 'Look at my tights. Ruined.'

'I expect he thought it was a game,' said Felicia. 'All that flapping. I'll replace them, of course.'

'You'll never pay off your mortgage at this rate.'

'You naughty cat,' said Felicia later. 'You're costing me a fortune. All those pot plants last week, and the net curtains and now Mary's tights.' Mog turned a gaze of pure innocent devotion and dumb imbecility towards her. He also switched on a two-stroke purr. It always worked. She scooped him up into her arms and staggered to the sofa under the weight.

'I'm really going to have to put you on a diet.'

This was not a word that figured in Mog's dialogue. His vocabulary reached four words on a good day. They were ME, FOOD, IN and OUT. He understood a great deal more, far more than he let on, but on a bad day he didn't understand anything. Mog had what Felicia called his 'deaf look'.

He put his deaf look on now.

The diet was not a good idea. Mog's irritability grew in direct inverse proportion with the decline in feeding. Felicia took to wearing thick gloves and wellington boots at his meal times. Otherwise Mog would attack her feet, pouncing on bare toes as she opened tins, chopped measured portions of fish, liver. Then he would grab her wrist with both paws in an iron grip to pull down the proffered dish of food.

If there were no seconds, he would corner her, growling, tail lashing, terrorizing her into submission. With great presence of mind, Felicia would divert his attention with a wide scattering of cat biscuits and escape upstairs.

'I refuse to be scared of my own cat,' she told herself in the bathroom mirror, her breath steaming the glass like Scotch mist.

The search for food turned into a twenty-four-hour obsession. Mog turned his attention to the neighbours. He observed their habits and meal times. He knew to the minute when Mrs Smith would take the shepherd's pie from the oven and then turn to dish up the vegetables. He logged the young Fosters' Friday night pizzas and had it out of the box before you could say pepperoni. Even baby food was not to be sniffed at ... he loved liver casserole, custard, lamb hotpot. There were lots of babies living in the road. They were always hungry too: even hungrier after Mog had dropped in for his share, howling their dismay as he exacted his price for peace.

It worked. The mothers could not cope with howling infants and savage cats at the same time. Mog swaggered home, custard on his whiskers, wondering how he could extend this form of extortion.

The next morning Felicia gave him the now insulting daily half-a-spoonful of catfood and three drops of milk and water. He walked all over it and tipped up the milk, leaving a soggy pond on the floor.

She raged at him. 'I've got all this to clear up before I go to work, you horror. I shall be late.'

Mog put his nose in the air and stalked off, offended. It

was not his fault. It was her fault. He shrugged loose any guilt on her doorstep and set off to commence his campaign of terror at the shops.

The supermarket was on the corner of the high street and he did not have to cross a road to reach it. He sniffed around the backyard cautiously. This was foreign territory. There were lots of black plastic bags and crates that smelt enticingly of food. He strolled inside as if he owned the place, temporarily awed by the army of feet and trollies. In a few weeks, he did own the place. He had only to skitter along a few shelves, sending packets, tins and bottles flying like skittles and he was put out the back with half a cooked chicken for his trouble.

The picture framer's next door was more of a puzzle till Mog discovered that sitting on and scratching a few prints left out on the counter for framing resulted in a hasty saucer of milk. The fish and chip shop was a piece of cake. The staff shrieked hygiene regulations and sent him packing with a handsome slab of haddock.

He had the smallest twinge of guilt in the china shop. The odds were so uneven. They couldn't catch him. The assistants daren't shout at him for the sake of the valuable bone china tea sets and expensive crystal glasses rattling tremulously on the shelves.

'Here, here, nice pussy,' they coaxed in low, panic-stricken voices. 'Nice biscuit, nice lump of sugar . . .'

Mog nimble-footed the Lladro till they offered nice ham sandwiches and then he jumped down and fled with lunch hanging from his mouth like a pink flannel.

Woolworths was just too big a target. He skated up and down the aisles, unable to get a grip on anything. He slunk away, growling revenge on the smart young manager, vowing war to the end, planning guerrilla raids and an all-out blitz.

In comparison, the classy dress boutique was a peach. Mog sat on an expensive black gown in the window, leaving his fawn hairs everywhere whilst thoughtfully chewing the sequins. They threw up their manicured hands in despair and went out to buy smoked mackerel and a Chubb lock.

If he couldn't get in then he discovered how to set off alarm systems. This was highly effective. The bank went berserk after the fifth alarm on the same morning. They pooled their lunches and lured Mog away from the premises with a trail of crisps, pork pies and cottage cheese. He ate himself horizontal.

Mog was not stupid. He realized that his cat-flap had shrunk and even tipping himself in, nose first, was becoming a problem. He waited outside in the growing dusk for Felicia to return from the library, greeting her with insincere purrs and rapturous ankle rubbing.

'I don't understand why you're not losing weight,' she said, putting the kettle on for a cup of tea. 'You're eating hardly anything.'

Mog agreed. Hardly anything at all. Not enough to keep a flea alive. He limped pathetically into the kitchen, too weak to do more than drag his magnificent tail along the floor. He planted his girth firmly in front of the refrigerator door and waited for the moment to pounce when Felicia went to fetch the milk.

Felicia wondered how to effect a trade-off. She wanted milk for her tea. Mog wanted his supper. Also in the refrigerator was her supper, a few succulent slices of cold chicken. She knew that one whiff of these and Mog would become an uncontrollable, savage jungle cat on the attack, intent on feeding a whole tribe of imaginary and starving cubs.

'Oh look,' she said casually. 'How careless of me. I've dropped a piece of fruit cake.'

As Mog pounced on a sultana, Felicia leaped at the refrigerator door and the bottle of milk was out in three seconds flat. She leaned against the counter, panting. 'This is getting ridiculous,' she murmured.

By late evening Mog was replete and had shed his mafia role. He flopped beside Felicia on the sofa and flaked out, four paws in the air, the pale fur of his underbelly inviting her tickly fingers. She buried her face in the soft powder-puff knowing she could trust him when he was relaxed.

Felicia sighed. Mog was a paradox. He looked so harmless when he was asleep.

The crunch came when Felicia stayed at home one day with a bad cold. Mog had to use the shrinking cat-flap. He had completed a successful persecution tour of the shops, collecting his pay-offs. He staggered home, growling ferociously at dogs, giving a young robin a nervous breakdown, savaging an unaccompanied basket of shopping briefly left in an open car.

Mog paddled wildly, trying to heave his great bulk through the aperture. He tried to retreat. He tried to use his considerable strength for a final launch forwards. But nothing happened, except an uncomfortable tight feeling around his middle that threatened to squeeze the breath out of him.

He was stuck.

Felicia found him when she came downstairs to fill her hot water bottle and make a drink. She turned away so that Mog would not see her laughing. She knew that cats, especially ones as proud as Mog, hated being laughed at.

She put on her gloves, tucked her pyjamas into wellington boots and gripped him round the middle in a purposeful fashion.

'If you dare scratch me, I'll leave you there all night,' she threatened. 'Now . . . one, two, three . . . heave.'

The next morning she took herself and her cold and Mog in a wire basket to the vet's. Mog chewed on the mesh like a hardened jailbird. He spat at all the quivering animals in the waiting room, fangs dripping with malice.

The vet paled and backed into a corner.

'Good Lord,' he said. 'You've brought Mafia Mog.'

Felicia looked bewildered. 'Excuse me, I don't understand?'

'This is the cat that has been terrorizing the neighbourhood. Not a shop has escaped his fiendish intimidation. He exerts pressure on fearful assistants the length and breadth of the high street.'

'I'm sure you must be mistaken,' said Felicia. 'He's . . . he's a very lovable cat,' she added, swiftly dodging a pair of unsheathed claws. 'He just needs to go on a diet.'

'I think we might be able to find a padded cell,' said the vet, suddenly noticing her streaming eyes. He offered her a clean handkerchief.

'I've got a cold,' she said.

'Vitamin C,' he suggested. 'Five hundred mgs.'

The GRMA thought that Mog had been sent to a penal colony in the remote outback of Australia. They spent their funds on sherry and prawn crackers and held a party to celebrate.

Felicia visited Mog twice a day. At first he would not look, pretending he did not recognize her, sitting with his back to the world. His padded cell was a centrally-heated apartment with a good outside run and his own tree. The bill was going to be considerable. Mog had chewed up his blanket and sat among the debris with a wounded expression.

'He has to learn that unsocial behaviour is not acceptable,' said James Hadlow, the vet. 'How's your cold?'

She saw James almost as frequently as she saw Mog and they discussed Mog's antisocial behaviour at length. James was studying animal psychology – 'the science of nature' – and Mog fascinated him. So did his fragile owner with her gossamer hair and cornflower blue eyes, now clouded with worry.

'If I didn't know you, Felicia,' said James, 'I would say that Mog lacks owner-attention and tender loving care.'

'Lacks owner-attention, indeed. How unfair,' Felicia objected. 'I lavish hours on the ungrateful beast.'

'I know. There must be some other reason.'

Mog returned home after two weeks on a strict low-calorie diet, sleek and fitter than ever. He felt fit enough to take on Woolworths. He was more magnificent than ever now his circumference no longer equalled his length. Felicia wondered cautiously if this new slim-line Mog planned on picking up his mafia connections.

He did. The shops, lulled into complacency by his absence, had let their security drop. He had a spectacular day, striking terror into the commercial heart of the high street. Even Woolworths capitulated when he was discovered putting the pick-and-mix all over the floor like a Golf Open Champion.

Felicia arrived home to a flood of complaints. Mog had also tipped over several seed boxes, danced a fandango on a newly laid cement drive and gone fishing in a neighbour's pond.

She phoned James, distraught. 'I don't know what to do.'

'Give me an hour,' he said.

Felicia waited apprehensively. She loved her cat. She just wanted him to be a little more docile.

The quietness of the evening was suddenly shattered by the roar of a powerful motorbike, all cylinders blasting. It stopped outside Felicia's house. A giant in tight black leather trousers and black studded jacket heaved himself off the machine. He was an awesome sight in black leather boots with spurs and a huge black helmet with a visor covering his face.

Mog stared, aghast, then turned to make a swift retreat. But the giant moved faster.

'Oh no, you don't,' he said in a sinister hissing voice, swooping him up with hands encased in gauntlets. 'In future, if you don't behave, this is where you are going.'

He opened the panniers on the powerful 1,000 cc bike and showed Mog the dark cavernous interiors. Mog shuddered at the thought of those shadowy holes.

'These are the sin-bins for extortionists, for cats with criminal activities who are not fit to be owned by nice young women who work in libraries, like Felicia.' Mog cringed. 'And I shall have no compunction about sentencing you to an hour's solitary in a sin-bin every day if you continue your present antisocial mode of behaviour.'

Mog froze in midair. He was thoroughly alarmed. He

had no doubt that this black leather giant with a helmet for a head would carry out his threat. He felt a glimmer of respect for the creature.

'From now on, I'm in charge,' the stranger growled.

Mog hung his head.

James took off his helmet in Felicia's kitchen and accepted a cup of coffee. 'It's authority Mog needs,' he said. 'You have always been too nice to him. Now he knows that there's a big black leather-clad stranger in charge, perhaps his behaviour will change. I can borrow my brother's gear any time.'

'I'm impressed,' said Felicia.

'I have given a deal of thought to Mog's behaviour. I think he's bored and lonely.' James slightly emphasized the word lonely. 'He needs a companion. Despite being solitary creatures, I believe that cats should always be kept in twos.'

'You mean I should get another cat?'

'I think a lively kitten would keep Mog on his toes. He would be so busy defending his own territory that he would not have time to go marauding.'

'I'll do that. I'd love another kitten.'

'Vets get lonely too, and I think I'm falling in love with you, Felicia,' said James, hesitantly. 'I can cope with two cats, even when one of them is Mog.' He could not stop himself from taking her in his arms. She went willingly with a husky sob of delight, longing for his closeness.

Mog growled. He wondered how all this lovey-dovey stuff would affect him. He had a feeling that his mafia connection was being severed for ever, but he was not too dismayed. He fancied a ride on that superlatively powerful bike, through not in a pannier. Wow, it would be transcendent . . .

THE BOND

The black cat shivered among a coil of salt-soaked rope, curled in mute misery as the boat heaved and rolled in a peculiar four-way motion that was both sickening and alarming.

The wind swept a cloud of rain into the cat's eyes, drenching them with tears, something he knew nothing about.

It was a barren shoe-shaped straggle of rock with a limestone plain, thin soil and no protection from winter winds. The salt dried under the summer sun in two large lagoons and any water on the island was brown and briny. The land rose at the toe and heel of the shoe and wild rosemary flourished on the hills.

There were wild pigs and asses on the island but no cats.

It was catless. There was no way that cats could cross the turbulent channel that separated the small island from its larger inhabited sisters.

The first cat came by boat across Los Freos, the rough channel between Ibiza and Frumentum, the given Roman name of the smaller island. It was a local fishing boat that had blown off course and found itself in the dangerous cross currents, surrounded by submerged rocks and tiny islets that might tear apart the hull of the old wooden boat in minutes.

For a moment the boat steadied in calmer waters near the salt lagoons and the cat's ears pricked up at the change of tone and his whiskers twitched. He smelled land. He had had enough of sea-faring. He had worked hard to keep the boat free of rats for a few scraps of food. He glimpsed a haze of land on the horizon, flat and windswept, and without hesitating he leaped overboard. The cat sank into the churning depths then surfaced, paws thrust through the water, a lean black otter shape fighting for survival.

Caught in the same squall, a pirate ship made ready to beach on the southern shore, scraping its hull on the rocks that were hidden in the treacherous weed-infested shallows. The men jumped into the swirling seas, their rough voices shouting to each other as they struggled ashore.

The corsair captain had a female cat that lived in his cabin and kept it sweeter smelling by catching mice. The man hesitated on the creaking heaving deck; he had no feeling for people – he killed and they died – but a watery grave held horror for him and it was a pretty grey-striped female cat with appealing ways. On impulse he went back to his cabin and tucked the animal inside his full-bloused shirt. As he struggled ashore the heavy seas hit him in the back and he fell, hitting his head on a rock. The cat clawed and fought to escape from the smothering weight of the man's body. She slithered free and raced across the sand, thin and fast as a whippet, climbing the low cliffs until she could crouch in some shelter beneath the gnarled branches of an olive tree.

When she had recovered from the shock of the wreck, she ventured into the hills, exploring her new environment. She found a narrow slanting hole in the hillside and, curious, eased herself in cautiously. She could see in the gloom. After a few metres of vertical descent, the hole levelled into a passageway which led to a cool and dry cave. Fallen bracken crackled under her paws.

She slept for a long time, exhausted. When she awoke a pair of gleaming yellow eyes were glinting at her in the darkness of the cave. A lean black shape approached her.

Sixty-five days later, she felt a weariness coming over her as she padded restlessly round the floor of the cave. She pushed the dry bracken into mounds and trampled on it. She began to growl softly and looked around in an agitated and puzzled way. She had no understanding of these strange feelings and was not aware of what was happening.

The black tom watched her, also disturbed by her restlessness. They had a tenuous unspoken bond but still he left to go hunting. There were colonies of small jade-green lizards sunning themselves on the rocks, and although they were not a favourite food they were slow and easy to catch. Later he would go to the shallows and fish. The sea was warmer now and he did not mind if his paws got wet or he fell in. He was becoming a sea cat. He could swim strongly and his powerful claws could catch a fish and dash its head against a rock in one swoop.

Living on the island suited both shipwrecked cats. They

had filled out and their coats had taken on a silken sheen. Their diet was more varied than ship-board scraps; they hunted for birds, insects, mice and fish.

Dried heather lay hidden among the bracken. The female cat stretched herself, crushing the small sweet flowers, and waited. Fierce spasms began to ripple down her flanks and she contracted her claws, quietly growling to herself.

She sat up when the head of the first kitten was presented and pushed it out. The tiny creature lay inert and she licked it hard with her rough tongue, removing the amniotic sac and forcing air into its lungs. She ate the placenta quickly and then chewed along the chord.

When she had finished she rested for a while, but she did not have long before the pangs began again and another kitten was on the way.

As soon as the litter of four kittens was safely delivered the new mother cleaned herself, curled round them, gathering the babies close to her body, and went to sleep. She had never been so tired.

The feral tom returned with a fresh red mullet. He thought the kittens were vermin and would have eaten them, but she fought him, spitting and scratching. He crouched back, alarmed by her ferocity. She snatched part of the fish from him, ravenous. Each time he returned, she had to fight to protect her kittens' lives.

The kittens began to crawl and mew and suck from their mother. The tom was wide-eyed with curiosity. He kept a watchful eye on the female cat who was ready to sink her claws into him if he so much as opened his jaws. But now he was beginning to recognize them for what they were. There was one black kitten, like himself, two pale striped tabbies like the mother and a different one. This last kitten was pale, with clearly defined black spots and pointed tri-angular ears: she was a distinct strain of the Spanish Lynx, an Iberian mainland cat. She grew very long and sleek, with eyesight as keen as a hawk.

As soon as the kittens were old enough and strong enough to be left, the female came out of the cave. It was summer now and she took to the cliffs, hunting for the eggs of seabirds which she knew instinctively would be good for her. She was thin after feeding the insatiable kittens but the sun felt good on her body, and her legs took her quickly through the gorse and wild rosemary on to the cliffs where the birds nested.

It was not long before she regained her strength and the kittens grew adventurous and tumbled into the sunshine, fighting and biting and scratching. They began to hunt as a pack, four lean young cats streaking through the pine woods and thick scrubs, mostly at night, catching rabbits and rodents, spending the indolent days stretched out on the rocks asleep.

The corsair's cat and the fisherman's cat mated again and when a new litter of demanding kittens arrived she had almost forgotten her first family. They found other caves to live in. The bond was broken.

She was a good mother, instinctively protective, and taught her new babies how to hunt for birds and eggs and fish.

But with her third litter, the kittens did not survive. She ate them thoughtfully, not wasting the protein of her body. There had been a sudden heavy rainstorm that flooded the floor of the cave. She had been forced to perch uncomfortably on a small ledge of rock on which she could not turn or move; one by one the kittens suffocated. She knew there was another kitten to come. The spasms were getting weaker as she pushed and strained in the damp, dripping darkness but still the kitten did not appear. She began to tire.

The feral tom returned briefly. He knew something was wrong and fled. He mated with the dark spotted female with pointed ears and she raced away to the flat plain and the sand dunes that rose near the salt lagoons. Her long whiskers twitched at the salt in the air. She surprised a nest of storm petrels and nosed their reed-built nest into a burrow in the dunes. She would be warm and dry there. She snapped at some bright insects and lay down in the sandy hollow, her slit eyes glinting in the sunlight. She had no further need of the tom.

The first settlers were farmers lured by the prospect of a peaceful life on the small island away from invaders and pirates. The cats sat on the natural outcrop of rock that enclosed the salt lagoons and watched the men unloading farming implements and sacks of seed. The men called the island Frumentum when they discovered that they could grow good wheat in that climate, despite the light soil.

Gradually the wild cats were pushed back to the hills as the farmers and fishermen built small communities. Dry-stone walls sprang up over the plain and what had once been rain tracks became a myriad of rough paths crossing the island, stony and rocky, for the farmers leading their mules. Nor was it easy for the ferals to fish with boats drawn up on the shore and men toiling day and night. The cats reverted to night sorties, keeping to the hills by day, watching from hiding places when the women came to look for herbs and firewood. They did not reveal themselves. They did not trust these loud beings on two legs.

The farm cultivation brought about a change in the prey that the cats could catch. Chased into the hills, succeeding families of ferals forgot how to fish. They became very wild and hungry. Sometimes they raided a farm for poultry or the litter of a sow.

So the farmers brought over unclean, growling beasts which they let loose on the land to protect their stock. The cats hated these coarse, yapping creatures with yellowed teeth. If they got a chance they would jump on the back of a farm dog. It was easy to surprise a lazy enemy.

The ferals showed remarkable adaptability as Formentera moved from wheat-growing to tourism. It was a lot less work for the farmers to simply market the sun and the beaches.

At first the cats merely watched from their rocks and kept away from the excursion ferries that came across from the port of Ibiza. Los Feros was still unpredictably rough and the holidaymakers staggered ashore on weak legs and threw away their packed lunches.

The wild cats followed them at a distance, then more boldly. They were big cats, long and lean, grey-striped, spotted, panther black, with large pointed ears and sharp faces. They developed a taste for bread rolls, cheese and ham.

Their life pattern changed. They homed in on the tourists, took up summer residence near the three concrete hotels, sunning themselves on air-conditioning plants, scavenging among the kitchen refuse, begging on the verandas of the self-catering bungalows. They were not tame enough to touch but they fawned on the holidaymakers like corrupt courtiers at a seventeenth-century court ball.

But when October came and the holidaymakers departed to the mainland and further, the cats sped back to the hills, the caves and the hollows. They picked up their hunting skills and shrugged off any veneer of civilization. They took a last pack race through the main street of San Francisco Javier, the island's tiny capital, like a mob of gangsters leaving town. It was a yearly ritual.

Few saw the cats. The dusty main square was deserted except for some old women swathed in layers of black skirts and shawls and stiff straw hats. They came to sit outside cafés without being pestered by amateur photographers.

Jane was one of the last holidaymakers to leave. She was a student of archaeology and the island was teeming with historical sites despite having been abandoned to the wild ass and pigs for long periods. She wished Angus was more interested. He only wanted to spend his days balancing on a surfboard or dancing the evenings away in the disco.

'The caves of D'en Xeroni are spectacular,' she said on their first morning on the island. 'Are you coming with me?'

'I don't dig caves,' he said, grinning at his own joke.

'And there was a monastery built on La Mola in 1403. But it's vanished now.'

'So what? It's gone. Come down to the beach. That's where it's all happening.'

Jane wondered again why she was on holiday with Angus. He was good-looking, fun to be with and she needed him in bed. But that was all. She hated herself at times.

On the last afternoon of their holiday they quarrelled and Jane went to see a cave hidden in the hills. Angus refused to come. He was determined to go home leather brown.

She walked stiffly past old fig trees propped up all round by long staves, looking like medieval pavilions, creating a circle of shade wherein old legends were recounted.

Long-staved windmills and round watchtowers were other silent reminders of the past. Jane loved all these clues, so little was written down. The people even spoke a regional dialect of Catalan with expressions that were as archaic as the hills.

The twisting road led to the highest point of the island. It climbed through gorse and wild rosemary; Jane crushed the herb between her fingers and walked along inhaling the fragrance from the palm of her hand. As she climbed higher, the whole of the narrow length of the island was out-stretched below her, strips of pale sand on either coast, La Sabina and the salt lagoons in the far distance. It was all so quiet and beautiful; she wished Angus was with her.

The receptionist had told Jane that the cave was on the side of the road after the Café Mirado. It had a very narrow entrance and was hard to find.

Jane needed this time away from Angus. They would be returning to London the following day and she was con-fused. She wanted to think about the people who had once lived out their isolated lives on the island . . . find answers for her problems.

The solitary café stood among stunted fir trees on the highest curve of the hill. She was beginning to tire and did not want to be out on the hills when the sun went down. A small boy played on the steps of the café.

'Do you want a drink, senorita?' he asked.

'After the cave,' she said.

She almost walked past the cave. It was simply a slit in the rocky bank by the roadside. The entrance was not overgrown but rubbish had accumulated. Jane cleared away Coke cans and cigarette packets.

She surveyed the fissure in the rock. It did not look promising. She began to ease herself in backwards. Her feet suddenly dropped into nothingness and for a moment she was alarmed by the sense of hanging in midair.

Cautiously she moved back, her feet seeking some foothold. She was relieved when the hole broadened and she could slither, using knees and elbows to propel herself along. The passage began to level out and her body stopped descending. She crawled, finding room to turn round, the light from her flashlamp pinpointing the dusty rock face. It widened into a small cave.

The silence was eerie but Jane did not feel alone. There was nothing to suggest human occupation yet it did not feel barren or empty. A stillness echoed the beat of her heart. Her senses were very alert, nerves tingling.

She flashed the light round the cave, probing the darkness. Suddenly two pinpoints of light reflected back. She moved towards them and something small and grey took shape on a ledge in the depths of the cave. She climbed towards it and realized that it was a pale, grey-striped cat. It lay exhausted, small shudders rippling along its body.

'Hello,' said Jane, softly. 'What's the matter?'

She ran a hand along the cat's flank. There had been many litters of kittens at home and it was clear to see that this cat was in labour. She saw a kitten, half presented, butt end first, and it was quite stuck. The cat's breathing was shallow, her fur damp and wet as if it had rained recently. She must have been straining and pushing this awkward kitten for hours, perhaps days.

Jane put the flashlamp on a higher ledge and adjusted its

position so that she could see what she was doing. Common sense told her that a little manual persuasion might save the mother's life if not the kitten's. She took a handkerchief out of her hip pocket and put it gently over the tiny part of protruding kitten. The cat lifted her head at this movement and stared with yellow eyes. Memories of a dark-haired human stirred among the confusion of pain and anxiety. A man had once put her inside his bloused shirt and jumped into the raging sea. He had saved her. This human smelt different but she was speaking with a soft voice . . . in her pain, the corsair and the girl became the same person and the cat could feel again the beat of his heart and the warmth of his damp chest.

Jane gripped the end of the kitten with two fingers, firmly but gently. She knew it should not be pulled but eased out slowly when the cat strained again.

'Come on, little girl,' she urged. 'Just one more push.'

But there was no movement from the cat. Jane could not see the cat properly now that the narrow beam was focused on the kitten.

'Don't give up,' she whispered. 'Please, puss . . .'

She strained to catch the cat's breathing but all she could hear was her own. She peered into the gloom but saw only the flutter of her handkerchief.

The flashlight toppled on its side and the beam wavered wildly over the roof of the cave. Jane caught it before it fell. Her handkerchief fluttered to the ground. Perspiration trickled down her face. She had to get that kitten out or both the mother cat and the kitten would die.

But she must have light. She moved quietly but carefully, gathering stones to prop the lamp into position. The beam swung across the ledge where the grey cat had lain.

It was empty. There was nothing there. Jane moved the light to the ground to see if the cat had slipped off and fallen to the floor of the cave. But she saw only her own feet and dry heather and bracken swept in by the wind.

Her hand was shaking as she held the lamp. There was a scattering of white spread across the ledge. Jane peered closely, just making out the little bones. There were so many tiny ivory fragments, long, short, flat. The small skeleton lay at rest, untouched, undisturbed for centuries.

Jane moved back, a sob in her throat. She did not understand. It had been a living cat under her hand, real fur, feeling real pain. She had not imagined it. And for a few moments there had been a strange bond between them.

She made her way slowly to the surface. It was much easier climbing out and the late afternoon sunlight was warm and pleasant. Angus was sitting on the bank with two cans of Coke.

'Had enough of caves now?' he grinned. She smiled her thanks and crept into his comforting arms.

'This is one cave I would not have missed,' she said. 'It was special.'

Her hand closed over the handkerchief in her pocket. It was damp. And the next day, when she packed for home, she saw that a few silvery grey hairs clung to the white fabric.

SOMETHING FUNNY
IN THE ATTIC

Something fell into her outstretched hand. Jodie screamed. It was a small, brown, furry mouse, yet it was not exactly a mouse. She hated mice. If she had not stood frozen with fear, she would have thrown the thing away as far as possible.

In those first moments of indescribable horror, she stared at the creature. A tiny, teddy-bear face stared fearlessly back. A little nose began twitching. The creature clung on to the curved palm of her hand. The folded membranes at either side of the tiny body registered. It was not a mouse. It was a bat.

'Erg!' she shrieked with total revulsion. If there was one thing she hated more than mice, it was bats. They got into hair and Jodie had long auburn hair.

She could hear something else beyond her thudding heart. She peered more closely. The tiny bat was chattering; a minute squealing and hissing noise was coming from even tinier jaws. It was either angry or frightened, but its brain was definitely registering some emotion.

It was so unexpected that some of Jodie's fear went onto hold. How could she be scared of something so small that was also afraid of her or – even more ridiculously – something minute that was actually annoyed with her?

It was so small that she decided it must be a baby bat. She ought to do something, whatever fear she felt. After climbing carefully down the ladder-like steps from the attic, she deposited the bat carefully into an upturned tea cosy that still held the warmth of the pot. Minute claws clung to strands of bright wool.

'Now stay there,' said Jodie. 'While I phone somebody. I don't know what to do with you, do I?'

It took several calls to find the right somebody. Jodie spoke to the zoo, the Nature Conservation Society and eventually found the way to a Bat Group. She had not known that such a thing as Bat Groups existed.

'Can you help me? I've got something funny in the attic and a bat in my tea cosy.'

'Don't touch it,' a deep voice barked.

'Of course I'm not going to touch it,' said Jodie, exasperated by the man's tone. 'They're revolting. As if I would go around picking up bats for fun. It fell into my hand. Will you come and take it away?'

'Let's get this straight. They are not revolting. They are a protected species. Technically you can be fined up to £2,000 for handling one. You have to have a licence, even for taking a photograph.'

'No one is fining me £2,000,' said Jodie indignantly. 'It fell into my hand by itself. And I've no intention of taking photographs, even though it's a baby.'

'I'll be along right away. Don't disturb the others. There must be a mother around.'

Jodie smothered a shriek. 'The others? You're joking.'

She had moved into the oast house some weeks earlier. It was all part of a dream, to modernize and redecorate a challenging project; to make her name as an interior decorator with a four-page feature in a glossy magazine. Jodie made a good living gutting rabbit warrens and turning them into spacious open-plan offices with colour schemes that promoted a harmonious working atmosphere. She liked to think she added her own signature with carefully chosen plants and pictures, even mobiles. Her clients thought so; so did her employer, Geoffrey Donnelly.

'You bring in more commissions than anyone else,' he said paternally, though eyeing her auburn hair. 'I might even make you a partner.'

That'll be the day, thought Jodie.

So the oast house was special. She had a vision of split-level rooms, a spiral staircase, ceilings with concealed lighting and pivot lamps. The possibilities were endless. There were two round rooms above, one oblong room below, an octagonal cupboard that defied being transformed into a bathroom. The bad news was a damp passageway kitchen with an earthenware sink practically dating from the Middle Ages.

Jodie had not given bats a thought when she bought the oast house. Mice, woodworm, spiders ... she could cope with those with a few traps, clean sweeps and applications of chemical control.

The baby bat was crawling about in the tea cosy like an inquisitive infant. Jodie felt a strong desire to stroke the tiny furry head with her little finger, but remembering the bat handler's threat of a hefty fine she stuck her hands in the pockets of her jeans. She made herself some coffee to calm her nerves. She wished the expert would hurry up . . . the baby might be getting hungry.

The bat handler arrived; he was tall, lean-faced, craggy. He looked like a man who spent half his life in dark caves.

'Matthew Brand,' he said. 'You phoned about a bat.'

'Have you got a licence?' she retorted, still trying to cover her initial fright.

'Of course I have,' he snapped. He strode in. 'You have to be trained to handle bats or inspect roosts.'

'What a lot of fuss about a wild thing.'

'Necessary, I assure you. They are brutally ill-treated; people think they are vermin. The change in the environment is banishing them from their natural roosts and the use of chemicals and insecticides is killing them off.' Matthew Brand looked suspiciously at the photographic equipment in Jodie's chaotic sitting room. 'I hope you haven't been taking photographs.'

'Of course I haven't,' said Jodie with a groan of protest. 'I'm modernizing this oast house and taking before and after shots for publication.'

'Oh, a journalist,' he said dourly, as if he had personally suffered from too much media attention.

'An interior decorator,' Jodie corrected.

'In a tea cosy you said?' he asked.

'Pardon?'

'The bat?'

She led him through to the narrow kitchen. The artistic

possibilities of a photograph leaped at her. The little bat was peering over the crocheted edge of the tea cosy with round and curious eyes that held an alarming intelligence. It was making surprisingly lusty cries.

'Those are isolation cries. It's hoping its mother will come down and rescue it. And no, you can't take a photograph, however expensive the magazine,' he added, reading her thoughts.

There was no doubt the handler knew what he was doing. Jodie was fascinated by the gentleness of the examination; disturbed by the wiry dark hair on the back of his wrists. Geoffrey Donnelly was dark too, but he had no effect on her, none whatever, despite the persistence of his attentions.

'Seems to be unhurt, thanks to an expert catch. Good at rounders, were you? The little fellow's hungry. They soon get short of fluid. Have you got a paintbrush?'

'A paintbrush?' Jodie repeated like an idiot.

'Fine watercolour – not a two-inch distemper.'

Jodie was able to put her hands on her paintbox in seconds. Matthew Brand made up a small quantity of cow's milk and water, and with the tip of the clean paintbrush moistened the bat's mouth lightly. After a moment's hesitation, the tiny jaws opened and sucked in the liquid. Jodie was amazed at its pin-sharp little teeth.

'Will you feed it on anything?'

'Mealworms.'

Jodie immediately felt sick. 'Not here, I hope . . .'

'Or tinned cat food. If the mother fails to pick it up, I'll have to take junior away. Also I need to have a look at the roost.'

'I could feed the bat while you have a look around upstairs,' said Jodie. He looked at her as if she were totally incapable of such a delicate operation. 'I won't touch it, even if it gets into my hair.'

'That's a myth,' he grunted. 'They have perfect eye-sight. It's only because they fly so swiftly that people think they will get tangled in their hair.' He seemed to be considering Jodie's anxious face and deep hazel eyes. 'All right, you can carry on with the feeding, drop at a time; don't drown it in milk.'

Jodie glared at his tall back as Matthew Brand climbed into the boarded loft of the oast house. She turned her attention to the little teddy-bear face regarding her with absolute trust. Her heart did a somersault. This was ridiculous, she told herself; she hated bats.

'Here you are, baby,' she said softly, proffering the milky paintbrush. 'Have a little drink.' The tiny jaws opened and gobbled up the milk. How Geoffrey would have laughed at her and made belfry-type jokes.

'Yes, you've got bats,' the handler said, returning later with cobwebs in his dark hair and smudges on his face. 'A very nice roost. When the mother emerges tonight she may pick up the baby.'

Jodie shuddered. Perhaps she could phone Geoffrey and go out to dinner somewhere civilized. She didn't want to be around when the pick-up took place. But nor did she want to encourage Geoffrey.

Matthew put a well-wrapped hot-water bottle in the bottom of a cardboard shoe box and carried the baby in it up the ladder into the loft. Jodie felt exhausted by the drama of the afternoon and dismayed because she had not done a stroke of her own work.

'They're pipistrelles,' he went on. 'Britain's smallest bat and easily tamed.'

'I'd rather have a cat.'

'No cats allowed until your colony goes. Cats catch bats. No chemicals either. I presume you are planning to do something about all this wood?'

'Yes, and I'm going to remove part of the loft floor, expose those beautiful beams. I'm putting in a spiral staircase leading to a sleeping shelf.'

A shutter came down over his craggy face. 'You can't remove the loft floor. That'll ruin the roost,' he said darkly.

'But this is my house.'

'Not now, not entirely. Bats are shy, gentle creatures simply asking to be left alone. They are not aggressive and they never attack. They'll even get rid of your wood borers. Bats can eat up to three-thousand insects in a night.'

'Well, they haven't done too good a job up to now,' said Jodie, feeling she was being got at. 'Besides, I'm not going to feel very happy with all this nocturnal activity going on. I'm supposed to be making a professional name with this conversion. I don't want to spend my entire life revamping office typing pools.'

'I'm sorry if this causes a hiccup in your career, but could you really live with the destruction of such delicate and harmless little creatures on your conscience?'

'That's not fair,' Jodie fumed. 'You're making me sound like a murderess.'

'Precisely. Bats are the superstars of the animal world. Are you going to condemn this roost to death?'

Jodie felt like a criminal. She made herself and the brash bat handler some strong coffee and spilled coffee grains everywhere. Drat the man. Why did he have to come and spoil her dreams?

'I'll be back in the morning to see if the mother has picked up her baby,' he said as he left.

Jodie spent the night hearing noises and squeaks and flutterings. She pulled the sleeping bag over her head and huddled up on the comfortable sofa but sleep was a long time in coming. The bats seemed to have custody of her eyes. She imagined swift little shadows, shapes half seen in the moonlight. She thought of their secret world in her rafters, tiny shapes hanging upside down from the walls and roof, squeezed into cracks and cavities.

'They're not asking for much,' she mumbled to herself as she drifted into sleep at last.

The bats stayed. She could not face Matthew Brand's withering disapproval. She told him the next morning that she would change her conversion plans so that the loft remained untouched.

His keen, gleaming look was worth the sacrifice, but Jodie was only obeying an age-old instinct. She was drawn to Matthew Brand. Without touching her once, he had managed to make her very aware of him. If she needed bats in her attic to keep him around, then she would learn to like bats.

'And the baby?'

'We weren't too late. The mother has picked him up. They only have one baby at a time, that's why it's difficult for a colony to survive.'

'I'm glad,' said Jodie. 'I'm only here at weekends. It would have been a bit difficult feeding the baby.'

'Do you want to learn about bats?' Matthew asked suddenly.

She would have stood on her head for him. 'Yes,' she said bravely.

'Next weekend I'll show you some other roosts. You'll need waterproofs and wellingtons, a torch and a helmet.'

It was the first of many damp and uncomfortable weekends. Jodie climbed belfries and attics, explored caves and mines. Once Matthew let her stroke the furry head of a funny long-eared bat that had a torn membrane. It was as soft as thistledown. She was amazed at the minute stitching with which the vet had mended the tear.

Jodie grew fond of the little family in her rafters. She was never alone. She enjoyed shocking her friends by telling them she had bats in the attic. They either shrieked with horror or wanted to see them.

'I think all this country living has gone to your head,' said Geoffrey in an irritable voice. 'Why not give it up? You're not concentrating on our offices any more. Why, only last week you tried to persuade a client to have trees painted on the office walls.'

'The typists had nothing to look at but a warehouse.'

'It won't do, Jodie.'

Winter came and as British bats are not long-distance travellers Jodie's family in the attic had to hibernate. She missed their little friendly noises. Matthew had told her that they would store enough fat to keep them alive during their long sleep.

One night she awoke in the round room that was now a comfortable bedroom and heard familiar sounds. The bats were stirring. But they should still be fast asleep. It was frosty midwinter. The silent landscape was white. She phoned Matthew immediately.

'Something's wrong,' she said. 'The bats are moving about.'

'They can't be,' he said, wide awake although it was long before dawn.

'I'm not imagining it. I can hear them distinctly.'

There was a pause as Matthew considered the possibilities. 'What have you had done to the house recently?'

'The rewiring's been done and a new dampcourse. Oh yes, a heating engineer has put in the central heating.'

'Central heating!' he roared down the phone. 'They think it's spring! They'll starve. There's no food for them. Turn it off immediately.'

When Matthew arrived at the oast house, a muffled figure opened the door. Jodie was wearing three sweaters, a knitted hat and fur gloves and was still shivering. He took her into his arms.

'I love you,' he said tenderly. 'You've turned off the heating for the bats.'

'I must be mad,' said Jodie, putting her cold cheek against his unshaven face.

Upstairs in the dark rafters, tiny inner computers registered the downward plunge in temperature. A female bat with a good fat store still felt warm and moved to a cooler spot; some thin males moved to a warmer place. Their deep hibernation was under control again. Downstairs the situation was not computerized and rapidly getting out of control.

Matthew was kissing her in a way that was generating a great deal of heat. She could feel the thunder of his heart even through three sweaters.

'I'll get a licence,' he said. 'Which would you prefer, Jodie darling, marriage or bat?'

'Bat, of course. I'd like to have a licence to handle bats. How long will it take?'

'About two years,' he sighed, his face lost in her long auburn hair, his mouth marvelling at the sweet fragrance of her skin.

Jodie needed no further prompting as his arms closed round her again, unable to hide her real longing.

'In which case,' she murmured, 'I think we should get our priorities right and apply for both.'

THE FOX
(True Story)

The beacon at Gringley-on-the-Hill was the highest point in Nottinghamshire. It stood out from the surrounding flat countryside of that county and its neighbours, Lincolnshire and Yorkshire.

Lighting the beacon brought all the important news . . . wars, coronations, royal births. Rhoda had watched the distant glow many times from her home, awed that such great events were taking place in the world.

It was to this village, Gringley-on-the-Hill, that eight-year-old Rhoda had been sent. This was her great event. She was to stay with her Uncle and Aunt Arrand on the farm which her uncle rented on the Estate of the Duke of Portland. In the family it was the custom to call aunts and uncles by their surname and Rhoda would never have dreamed of being familiar. She was not certain if she even knew their Christian names.

She was sent in the role of comforter; a slight girl with long dark brown hair, rod straight, framing her serious young face like a silk curtain. Lizzie Arrand, the only daughter of the farmer and his wife, and about the same age as Rhoda, had died of a fever, and Aunt Arrand welcomed Rhoda for company to help relieve the sadness of their loss.

Rhoda had walked from her family home in Gunthorpe, a small riverside village six miles away. As she approached the farmhouse she stopped to peer through the iron railings of the vicarage garden and watch the peacocks.

'I've never seen such beautiful birds,' she breathed as the birds threw out their radiant feathers.

Across the road from the vicarage was the farmhouse where Rhoda would be staying. She would be able to see the birds quite often. It was an exciting thought.

The Gringley farm was a two-storey brick building with a fold-yard, stables, cowshed and pigsties. The kitchen was the heart of the farmhouse, with its stone-flagged floor, whitewashed brick walls thick enough for a child to hide in the wall cupboards, and big sash window, the sill crowded with plants and ornaments.

The large wooden kitchen table was scrubbed nearly white; the high-backed wooden settle had a solid base to protect feet from draughts; there was a wooden chair and three-legged stool, a pegged rag hearth rug and, dominating the kitchen, the massive cooking range.

The range was an enormous black structure with a boiler on one side of the firegrate and the oven on the other. It was the first thing that Rhoda noticed when she arrived, wrapped in her best raglan coat, her hair almost hidden under a woollen bonnet.

'I can see you're admiring my range,' said Aunt Arrand. 'That's your face in the fender. It's steel and I polish it till it's like a mirror. You can do that on Saturdays.'

Rhoda did not answer; she was wondering where she was going to sleep. Would she be sleeping in Lizzie's room? She hoped not.

Later she discovered that her aunt kept the small window of Lizzie's room open day and night because it faced the churchyard where Lizzie was buried, and she could not bear the thought of shutting her little daughter out.

Aunt Arrand gave Rhoda a different room, from the tiny window of which she could see the rolling purple-brown fields of her home. She was homesick for the wind and the flat lane and the long straight lanes hedged with honey-suckle, and the wayside flowers and butterflies in plenty.

The order of work on the farm involved a grand clean-up of the kitchen on Saturdays. The kitchen range was black-leaded until it shone, along with the steel fender, till that reached the mirror-like perfection expected by Aunt Arrand. The flagged floor was scoured and stoned, and the hearth whitened with pipeclay. The chores were wearisome but Rhoda had to help. The wooden table was made ready for Aunt Arrand's baking of a week's supply of bread.

Rhoda loved baking day. She loved the wholesome aroma of the yeast rising; she loved watching the capable hands of her aunt slapping and kneading; she loved the rows of loaves as they came from the oven, crusty brown and steaming. Aunt Arrand never made less than two-dozen loaves of bread, along with hot cakes, scones, fruit pies and tarts and sometimes a big fruit cake. The hot cakes were for Saturday tea. Saturday tea was special, with bloaters brought by Uncle Arrand from market and the flat round bread cakes, big as dinner plates, thick with home-made butter.

This particular Saturday morning, early in November, held an air of expectancy for Rhoda. Her aunt had told her that there was to be a hunt 'meet', something she had never seen before.

It was a bright though frosty morning and the trees were shedding their autumn gold. Uncle Arrand had put a wooden box against the wall that separated the farmyard from the churchyard so that Rhoda could watch the gathering of the 'meet'.

She stood on the box shivering with the cold and excitement. The great gleaming horses were arriving outside the White Hart Inn in the High Street, the riders in red coats known as hunting-pink, the women riders looking so elegant in green or black habits. The pack of thirty hounds milled around, their tails wagging frantically at the thought of the day's chase ahead.

Suddenly the hounds stopped running around and stood with their noses in the air. They could hear the approach of a carriage and knew from past experience its arrival would be a signal to begin the hunting. They began baying and Rhoda was alarmed by the uncanny sound.

'Whatever's happening?' she asked anxiously.

Aunt Arrand had come out into the yard for a breath of air. The heat in her kitchen was building up already. She had seen many a meet before, but still found the scene impressive. She also wanted to make sure Rhoda was standing safely on the box.

'That's the carriage of her Ladyship, the Duchess of Portland,' she said. 'Watch carefully and you'll see that she'll step out of the carriage directly on to the back of the horse. Look, they're drawing her horse up ready.'

Rhoda's eyes widened as the Duchess negotiated the tricky manoeuvre; she was a regal figure with billowing skirts and yards of black veiling caught in the breeze, but Rhoda could not see her face.

'What are they all drinking, Aunt?'

'It's called stirrup cup.'

'What's stirrup cup?'

'You ask too many questions, lass. They'll be away soon, so come on in. There's enough to do without us both standing out here.'

But Rhoda stayed where she was, tiptoeing on the box, her bare hands turning white with cold. The meet moved off, the horses' hooves echoing on the cobblestones, the riders' voices calling, then rang out the Master of the Hunt's horn. The clear clarion notes sent a quiver of apprehension down Rhoda's spine.

'Oh, isn't it exciting,' she breathed.

'Aye, it's exciting all right,' said Aunt Arrand. 'But not for the fox.'

Aunt Arrand was not a tall woman. She wore a dark blouse and long skirt with a spotless, starched white pinafore for her baking. Her greying hair was screwed up tightly in a bun. She had a cotton cap on to keep the stray hairs off her face. Already her homely features were shining pink with the heat from the stove.

Rhoda wore her Saturday woollen dress with a tidy cotton pinafore over it, long woollen stockings and boots. She also had a dress for school and a dress for Sundays. She was very lucky, but they would be passed down to her sisters so it was an economical outlay.

As the day wore on, the chores were completed and the bread baked. It was a grand sight, the table covered with loaves left to cool. Rhoda had made a loaf too, smaller and misshapen because it had not fitted the bread tin, but she was proud of it. Proud as a peacock, she said to herself. She longed for the moment when her aunt would nod and smile and let her bite off a crust with her strong teeth.

The fire which had been stoked up to keep the oven hot for the baking was now left to quieten down. The oven door was left open to allow the oven to cool.

Aunt Arrand sat on the settle and put her feet on the stool. She sighed with relief.

'Make us a cup of tea, lass. We've earned it,' she said. 'Your loaf looks good. You're going to make some young man a good wife some day, Rhoda.'

Rhoda turned away to make the tea. Her life was already planned for her. She would take a place as a housemaid at one of the big houses and when she was eighteen or so she would marry a farmer, or a farm labourer saving to buy his own land. But there were other thoughts in Rhoda's head, even at eight. She liked reading; she liked inventing stories; she liked numbers and could add up faster than her teacher. Surely there was more she could do in life than black-lead a kitchen range and wash flagstones?

It was later in the afternoon when Aunt Arrand was beginning to think about clearing the bread away into the deep wall cupboards, and getting tea ready, that they both heard a great commotion outside.

Rhoda ran to the window. It was the hunt back again and in their backyard. A mêlée of hunters and hounds wheeled around the yard, the horses stamping impatiently, steam blowing from their nostrils, flanks heaving.

Rhoda gasped with astonishment. Her eyes widened, taking in every aspect of the scene. It was even more astonishing than the peacocks.

'Aye, what's all this?' exclaimed Aunt Arrand. 'What are they doing in our yard?'

She had hardly turned round from the table when suddenly a wet, weary and bedraggled fox appeared in the doorway. His desperate amber eyes looked straight at the two humans. His muddied russet tail swept the floor with an exhausted movement. Rhoda caught her breath.

The fox sloped past her and jumped straight into the open oven. In a flash, Aunt Arrand slammed the oven door shut and stood in front of it. At that moment the hounds caught the scent again and bounded into the kitchen in pursuit.

It was pandemonium. Rhoda jumped on to the stool, holding her skirts up from their muddy paws and wet noses. They ran round the kitchen sniffing everything, including the newly baked bread on the table. They approached the stove but the wave of heat drove them back. Aunt Arrand did not move.

The Master of the Hunt strode into the kitchen. He was a tall man and he was furious. He waded through the dogs, flicking his whip impatiently on his thighs.

'Where's that damned fox?' he barked like one of his hounds. 'It's here somewhere. I saw it. Speak woman, where did it go?'

'Tell your filthy dogs to leave my bread alone,' said Aunt Arrand, ignoring his questions. 'I don't want my bread sniffed at by a lot of muddy hounds. And look at my floor, if you please!'

'Damn your floor, woman. Where's the fox? They know it's here. They can smell it,' roared the Master.

'It took my niece Rhoda and I two hours this morning to scour this floor. Look at it now. Reckon it'll have to be done over. I'll thank you to get your hounds out of here,' Aunt Arrand insisted.

A youth was standing in the doorway. It was Farrow Gabertus. It was his first hunt. He would be bloodied when they caught the fox. His eyes were bright with the thrill of the fast chase and now the expected moment of the kill.

Farrow looked at the girl on the stool, holding her skirts close to her legs. He'd seen her before, peering over the churchyard wall at the vicar's peacocks. He knew she was Rhoda Robinson from Gunthorpe, come to keep her aunt company. He knew everything. He had an enquiring mind.

'A whole day's hunting and no fox at the end,' blustered the Master angrily. 'And all you can think of is your kitchen floor!'

He wheeled round and saw Rhoda standing on the stool, her smooth dark hair hanging down past her shoulders, her clear brown eyes regarding him with a directness that was unusual in a child.

'Now then, young lady. Perhaps you'll tell me, since this woman can only talk about her floor. I'm sure a bright little thing like you saw where the fox went.'

The Master of the Hunt was a tall man, but the stool gave Rhoda added height and she stared back.

'Come on, girl. Lost your tongue, have you? Perhaps this'll loosen it.'

He dug into his waistcoat pocket and pulled out a penny. He held the coin towards Rhoda. It glinted in the firelight like something touched with magic. Rhoda looked at it – and beyond. She saw the book it would buy, the ribbons or bit of lawn for a new handkerchief, but chiefly the book.

'Come on, girl, speak. What's the matter with the girl?
Is she dumb?' He glared.

The magical visions faded ... instead she saw the long
droop of that beautiful tail, the desperate eyes and weary
gait. She saw its awful slaughter in the kitchen by the greedy
hounds. She pursed her lips and ground her teeth closely
together. She would say nothing.

'Daft! Stupid lot of women. I'm losing my patience,' he
bellowed.

Aunt Arrand kept her place in front of the stove. She was
slowly getting hotter and hotter. Beads of perspiration broke
out on her forehead despite the chill from the open
doorway.

'Seems the fox is lost, sir,' said Farrow, speaking for the
first time. It was a squeaky light baritone. His voice was just
breaking. Rhoda kept her eyes down so that he would not
see her quick gleam of amusement.

'Dammit! Blasted wasted day. I don't know what her
Ladyship will say. Come on, Farrow.' The Master of the
Hunt strode out of the kitchen through the seething dogs,
calling the hounds off. They followed reluctantly, still
sniffing the ground, giving little yelps of disappointment.

Aunt Arrand waited until the horses had all cleared out
of the yard and the last sounds of hooves died away. She
wiped her neck and face with the edge of her apron.

'Better a roasted fox than a slaughtering in my kitchen,'
she said quietly.

She stood aside to open the oven door. It would not be
a pretty sight.

A beautiful rust-coloured animal, refreshed and rested,
jumped out of the oven and shook itself. The fox had dried
out and cleaned off all the mud. Without a glance it loped

out of the kitchen, across the yard and down the fields of Gringley-on-the-Hill into the wild woods beyond.

'Well, I never,' said Aunt Arrand. 'And it never stopped to say thank you. There's gratitude for you!'

But she was laughing. It was the first time Rhoda had seen her aunt laugh since Lizzie's death.

'Come on down off stool, lass. We've the kitchen to clean up again.'

When Uncle Arrand arrived back from market with the bloaters, he too laughed when he heard what had happened.

'He'll thank you by raiding your geese tonight,' he told his wife. But that was not so. Aunt Arrand did not lose any geese at all . . . that night or any other night.

Rhoda lived for periods with three other aunts. She was highly intelligent and always top of her class. She was fifteen when she came back to see Aunt Arrand. She had grown tall and had no need to stand on a box to watch the meet any more. Her hair was still long and straight and one day soon she would be expected to put it up.

Sometimes she was allowed to go on the cart with her Uncle Arrand to market; and this summer day she went to buy provisions for her aunt. Rhoda wore a dress of blue gingham and a freshly starched white pinafore. Before she left she tucked a wild daisy behind her ear.

The market was crowded with people and animals and stalls laden with produce. There was a man playing a pipe and gypsies selling handmade pegs and watercress. It was like a holiday and Rhoda's eyes lit up with anticipation.

She became aware of a young man staring at her. He was tall and lanky, his face tanned by hours of outdoor work, his eyes regarding her with recognition.

He came walking towards the cart and Rhoda felt her pulse quicken. She looked across for her uncle but he was talking to some other farmers with his back to her.

'Hello,' said the young man. 'You're the little girl who didn't want a special penny. Are you still watching the peacocks?'

Rhoda coloured. She knew who he was now. It was Farrow Gabertus, taller, broader, his voice settled into a deep Lincolnshire accent. But she said nothing. There was nothing she could say.

He looked at her boldly, his eyes glinting with amusement. 'I knew the fox was there, you know,' he said. 'I saw through the window. It hopped into your aunt's oven.'

Rhoda took a deep breath. 'Then why didn't you say something?' she asked, finding her voice at last.

'I had a choice,' said Farrow. 'Which did I want the most? The girl or the fox?'

He held out a strong, capable hand to help her down from the cart. Her soft hand fitted into his fingers like a glove. His smile had a burning sweetness that held her captive. It was like seeing the gorgeous plumage of the peacocks for the first time all over again.

'Mind you, Rhoda, I had to think twice,' he added.

The foxes often came to the ridge to look down on the farm, but one remembered and, with a short bark, he led the pack away into the hills, their tails streaming like fire.

WHITTINGTON

No one really knows if I existed or not. I belong to a ragbag of folklore that regards cats as lucky if you are kind to them but bad news if you kick them down the stairs.

They found my bones in his tomb. Not exactly bones, mummified remains in fact, but I don't like to think about that too much. I was much bigger than your cosy fire-side telly-watching twentieth-century moggy. I had longer legs and a larger body, more like a small dog. Blacky-brown, browny-black. My appearance would not make a calendar print.

There are three main avenues of confusion about my existence: merchants in those days talked of 'venturing' cats for a tricky cargo. French was spoken by educated traders in medieval times and the word for profit was *achat*. The slang word for a three-masted coal ship was a 'cat'. There you go, cat, cat, cat . . . it kept cropping up.

Richard Whittington, in whose tomb I was found, was a kind man, hard-working and industrious, and a public benefactor. In his will, he left one penny to every man, woman and child on the day of his death, though he did not make the perimeters clear; also forty shillings each week to be distributed among poor people existing in the ghastly prisons of London till £500 was spent. And more, much more . . .

He was four times Lord Mayor of London . . . not that being mayor means much to a cat. I only know that he suffered from the extreme cold of the winter of 1422 when the Thames was frozen over, and died in the March of 1423 during an epidemic of influenza. Being mayor did not make him immune.

We did not always rest in peace together. There was the Great Fire in 1666 and a flying bomb in 1944, both events devastating the church, and even a parson who robbed the tomb, taking the lead sheets which wrapped my poor master.

Richard did not start out being rich. He had to work long, hard hours for his board and keep. England was in a sorry state just before he was born. There had been that dreadful plague, the Black Death, which decimated the population, especially the townspeople. Before my time or I would have done my bit with the rats. Sometimes I can still hear the bells tolling for the dead.

There were not enough men for the work. No need for unemployment figures in those days for the polls and politicians. Quite the reverse. Not enough masons, apprentices, servants or farm labourers. Women had to work on the farms. Any efforts towards educating the poor were abandoned.

Dick Whittington came of gentry, third son of Sir William Whittington of Pauntley and Solers Hope, Herefordshire, with no prospects and an unhappy childhood at Coberley Hall. Maybe it was these sad years that gave him such compassion for all helpless creatures, poor things and poor people. Being the third son he did not inherit and came to London to be apprenticed to a mercer, Sir Ivo FitzWaryn. Poor bewildered lad, only thirteen years old, but glad of employment. Only the sons from honourable families were taken on as apprentices.

He had to pay two shillings and sixpence on entry and a further three shillings and fourpence on closure, some seven years later, so you can see that when he paid one penny for me in a street market, it was indeed a considerable sum for a cat.

I remember that fair and the waves of heat beating up from the ground on a hot, humid day. Oh, it was so hot. The fair was being held in a back lane near the Fleet, crowded with traders and idle strollers, such steaming humanity spilling out of all the alleyways. The ale sellers were busy, quenching the thirst of Londoners, selling ale that looked and smelt as if it were half Fleet water. The stench of all those people and animals was unbelievable.

The rush basket was stifling hot and I was dying for want of water. There was little shade either, as the trader had put me in front of the puppy dogs and hens and singing birds. I was but a few weeks old.

Dick was on his way to the mercer's house after relaying some errand, when he heard a squeak – my next to last squeak, I knew for sure.

'That kit's dying,' he said, pausing, wiping the sweat from his brow.

'Save it, s'r. You've got a kind face.'

'Aye, a kind face perhaps, but my home is far away in the country. I am an apprentice here in London.'

'One more cat in the kitchen of your master won't come amiss. Keep away the mice and the rats.'

Mindful of the plague, Dick reached into his purse for a small coin.

'One penny,' said the sharp trader, seeing the boy's eye soften with a rare compassion.

'One penny for a kit that will die on me in half an hour?'

I opened a dry, pink cavern of a mouth in feeble protest. I did not want to die. In seconds a penny had changed hands. It was a lot for those days. Even Dick thought of what he could have bought for a whole penny.

Dick poured some water from a leather pouch into his cap and pushed my face into it. Am I to be drowned now? my thoughts swam. But the water revived me, took away the heat of my fur, and soon I was drinking faster than my small, parched tongue could lap. I shall never forget the taste of that water in my master's cap, that held the taste of his skin, his hair, the dew from his pores.

He carried me back in his sleeve, uncaring of the wetness. I went to live in the kitchens of the merchant's house and earned my keep by keeping the mice down. My coat grew glossy and thick, and although I had no name I was always known as Dick's cat.

There were other apprentices and one of them was less than kind, who would kick me if he thought no one was looking. He had a mean face, bereft of humanity, with pinched nostrils and thin lips. He was jealous of Dick's good nature and his success in business matters.

I knew nothing about the good luck custom called venturing. My life revolved round eating and sleeping, hunting and hounding, finding young Dick for a few minutes' play with some yarn, or letting him stroke my thick fur.

The apprentices were given a chance of investing in something, like having a share in the ship that left England to trade with foreign parts. Richard was invited to venture in the *Unicorn*, soon to trade along the Barbary Coast, but he had nothing to venture and let the chance go by.

But the unkind apprentice, envious of the pleasure that Dick and I shared, had a plan.

I was asleep by the dying embers of the kitchen fire when suddenly a sack was thrown over me. I kicked and struggled and scratched wildly but the top was tied in a tight knot and I could only just breathe through the dust-encrusted mesh. The carrying, bumping and jolting almost shook my bones to pieces as I was taken somewhere.

It all smelt so strange and I cried out for Dick but he couldn't hear me. I sensed he was already miles away, working for our master, while his faithful friend was being borne to stranger places.

My surroundings moved and heaved, a horrendous rocking that sickened my stomach. I smelt new smells, salt and stench and ... I knew this smell ... rats.

A sailor heard my pitiful mewing and choking and let me out of the sack and soon I was a favourite on the ship. I missed my old life but since nothing could be done I made the best of my new circumstances, cleaning out the rats. I saw the dead being tossed over the side with great satisfaction.

'Isn't that Whittington's cat?' someone said, recognizing my marks and my prowess.

'He was too poor to venture anything so he ventured his cat, it seems.'

The trader began its bartering along the Barbary Coast and the Captain of the ship invited the local King and Queen aboard for dinner. The ship was anchored close to shore and in the commotion some uninvited guests also swarmed aboard for dinner.

When the meat course was being served to the royal pair, the rats appeared, eyes glinting with greed.

'Get the cat,' the Captain roared, horrified and embarrassed in front of his guests. But the royal couple were entranced by the way I set about the rats, pouncing and swiping, sinking my teeth into their necks. They wanted to buy me, offering a big casket of jewels.

'Our country is overrun with rats. This strange animal is valuable beyond any price,' said the Queen, touching my soft head with a royal finger.

The Captain explained that he could not sell me as I had been ventured by Dick Whittington. It was arranged that he should leave me behind while the ship traded along the coast, then pick me up before they began the return voyage.

I knew nothing of all this bargaining, only that once again I was in a strange humid place with an army of rats to defeat. There was sweet consolation in this foreign land . . . a small wild cat, streaked grey, and together we founded a new dynasty.

The time came to leave and I said goodbye to my tumbling kittens and reminded them of their duty. The King and Queen did not forget the casket of jewels and the Captain put it in his safe.

When we reached London at last and sailed up the bustling Thames, my fur was quivering with excitement. It would be good to be back in London. I could not wait to see my home and Dick again. I flew off the ship and raced up Leadenhall Street, tail high, but my master was not there. I could not find him anywhere.

Alice FitzWaryn, the merchant's daughter, was crying gently. 'He's gone, he's gone,' she said, wetting my fur. 'And it's all because of me.'

I struggled out of her arms and, picking up the scent, followed the steps of the young man. I found him some miles out of London, at the foot of Highgate Hill, sitting by a milestone, his head in his hands. It was a sad sight. He looked so distraught.

'It's hopeless,' he groaned. 'I'll never be good enough to marry her. Her father will never consent.'

How could I, a cat, tell him that his beloved wept also, and that a casket of jewels awaited him in safe-keeping? I could only twist myself round his ankles and nudge at his chin, and stand with my paws on his knees, kneading and purring. I felt so helpless. I prayed for help.

'Well, cat, at least you're pleased to see me,' he said, absent-mindedly fondling my ears. 'I've missed you.'

Then we heard Bow Bells ringing on the air, their joyous message resounding in our ears. They said something to both of us, reaching deeply into our veins, to our nerve ends. The message of all bells. God's human voice on this earth.

All the rest is history.

Dick was twenty-two when he opened his London shop selling velvets and damask, silk and wool, to the wealthy. The royal family were among his regular customers. He served three kings – Richard II, Henry IV and Henry V. Real money started to roll in when he sold two garments of gold to the King and made wedding dresses for Henry IV's two daughters.

He became Banker to the King, lending him huge sums of money, thousands of marks for various wars. He married his Alice and became Lord Mayor of London four times, then MP for London in 1416. He was a good man with immense power, both politically and in trade.

When he died he left instructions that all debts to him should be cancelled. He also left money – to build Whittington College, a hospital and almshouses; to construct a new Newgate gaol to a proper standard; for repairs to St Bartholomew's Hospital in Smithfield and a new library; to repair, glaze and pave the Guildhall and build another new library; and to construct a new West Gate into the City.

I had gone by then, worn out by my life of industry, but my many offspring served him well. Richard Whittington had owned a house in Gloucester. During repairs to the house in 1862, they found a figure of a boy carrying a cat. It was discovered under the stone floor of the cellar.

Now we are sealed together in cement in a common grave under the church floor of the rebuilt St Michael Paternoster Royal in Paternoster Lane. A woman who cares about cats came recently and put her hand on the cold stone. I could feel the warmth of her love intensifying and reaching down to my stiff and ancient fur. She spoke, soft and low. 'I'm sure you existed,' she said.

I wanted to tell her but what could I do? How could I

reach her mind and tell her my story, show her the evidence of my existence?

But I tried. And my thoughts led her to these words.

TOPPER

When Emma Carlisle moved into Stone Bank Cottage, she did not know that Topper went with it. Stone Bank Cottage was not a traditional roses-round-the-door type cottage; it was an undistinguished stone-walled house with a steep slate roof, lost halfway down an isolated lane.

The estate agent's blurb accurately measured the tiny rooms, the primitive facilities, the garden full of character – overgrown weeds, in other words. It made no mention of Topper either.

Emma had been searching for a retreat for months. After a decade of working in a big publishing company Emma grabbed at the six-month sabbatical they offered. It was the perfect opportunity to write the book that had been struggling for existence. She wanted to write a history of knitting.

It was hopeless to think of writing the book while working full time or living in her small London flat. There were too many distractions: friends phoning and dropping by, a film to see, a first night that should not be missed. She knew she ought to cut herself off from everyone and everything.

Stone Bank Cottage was far enough out in the country to discourage any casual calling of her friends, and sufficiently off the beaten track to make it improbable that anyone could find her.

Her love affair with knitting began in her early teens when she was confined to bed with a virulent bout of influenza; she was bored and restless, marooned upstairs, too headachy to read. Her mother stuck two needles and a ball of bright wool into her hands.

'Will you knit a blanket square, Emma? The Women's Institute are making wool blankets for refugees. Cast on thirty-six stitches and knit a six-inch square,' said her mother.

'Cast on thirty-six stitches? You're joking,' said Emma weakly. 'I don't know how.'

'Whatever do they teach you at that school?' Her mother took up the wool and made the first loop. 'Watch.'

Once Emma got started, she found she could not stop. By the time she was up and about, she was completely hooked. She knitted not one square, but eighteen, the last in a diagonal basket stitch she invented herself. From then on she was rarely seen without a pair of needles sticking out of her blazer pocket. She got a place at an art college and took a Design and Craft Course. Her favourite magazine ran a knitting competition which Emma won with a deceptively simple design for a Mexican poncho. When she went to collect her prize, Emma dropped hints the size of ostrich eggs that she was looking for a job.

Several weeks later she received a letter saying that there was a junior post vacant in the readers' enquiries department. Emma jumped at it. Any door was an open door. She worked hard and it led to transfers and promotions.

When she was appointed Craft Editor, Emma came across the word *cnyttan*. It was the Anglo-Saxon word for knitting, to tie or to knot. The word became a flame in her heart. Suddenly it was a whole history of women providing for their menfolk and families. She spent every spare moment poring over books and ladies' magazines and periodicals, delving back into the origins of knitting and development of patterns.

Emma signed the lease for Stone Bank Cottage and packed the filing cabinet of notes she had collected over the years. She borrowed an electric typewriter, bought a large stock of coffee and instant soup, and took herself off to hibernate for the season.

On her first evening she made a plate of toasted cheese and settled on the floor to sort through the enormous stack of papers which she had brought with her. Knitting was older than written history, beginning when men first got the idea of knotting grasses to make into nets, mats and baskets. The Scots were the first people to use wool.

Tap, tap. Emma looked up from a fascinating photo of fourth-century knitted wool socks. Tap, tap. The noise came again. It must be a branch tapping on the window. She would have to get used to country noises.

Emma began rewriting a few paragraphs on the 1571 Cappers' Act. This act laid down that every person above the age of six (excepting maids, ladies, gentlewomen, noblemen, lords, knights and gentlemen owning twenty marks' of land) should wear on Sundays and holidays a cap of thick wool made and dressed in England. The fine (or pain) for not doing so was 3s. 4d. It was difficult to put this old law into plain English, so she did not hear the next few impatient taps.

She looked around for inspiration and found herself caught in the gaze of two saucer-wide eyes staring at her through the window pane. A fat little body danced along the outside windowsill, tapping the window with unconcealed curiosity. It was a tawny owl.

Emma was not a country person and to her all owls were fierce beaked creatures who swooped on to defenceless mice and ate them whole. But this little creature was nothing like the predators she imagined. He was quivering with inquisitiveness, asking to be let in as if it were the most normal thing in the world.

Cautiously she opened the window and peered outside.

'Go away,' she said.

The owl instantly hopped inside on to the back of the sofa and scuttled down on to the floor, his head on one side as he perused the piles of paper. Nod, nod, very interesting, he indicated. He picked up a piece and began to shred it.

'No, please. That's important!'

Emma pounced on a drawing of William Lee's 1589 first-invented knitting machine and put it safely in a box file. The owl flew swiftly to the top of the standard lamp, hurt and astonished at Emma's antisocial action.

'Coo,' he muttered.

Emma handed him a sheet of scrap paper. 'You can tear this up instead.'

He reached out a tentative claw to grasp it. He tested it gingerly with his beak in case it was a trap. Finding it to his liking, he began to shred it into ticker-tape that floated serenely to the carpet.

'So you've met Topper,' said a voice through the window. 'Shall I take him away before he disgraces himself?'

Emma was glad that the voice was cool and distant; till her book was finished men were to play no part in her life.

'Topper? Do you mean to say this creature who is taking my home to pieces actually has a name?' she asked, equally cool.

'Of course he has a name. He's a long way up the evolutionary ladder; far removed from earthworms, etc. And it's not your home. It's actually mine. I'm Daniel Masters, owner.'

He stooped in a familiar way to duck under the beam over the front door, without asking if he could come in. He was a slim, rangey man, dark-faced, leaning heavily on a stick.

'I didn't know you were around,' said Emma. 'The agents told me you were climbing the Himalayas.'

'I was climbing Annapurna in Nepal with a party of Australians. Unfortunately I fell. My descent was rather rapid and I broke some bones in my foot.'

It sounded like an understatement. His foot was in plaster and a thick sock.

'How awful,' said Emma. 'Will you want your cottage?'

'No, you can stay at Stone Bank. I'm recuperating with mother at the Lodge. It's Topper I'm worried about.'

'Worried about an owl?'

'Topper's confused. He's lived with me since he was a chick. While I made my preparations for the climb I gradually encouraged him to live wild in the woods. I never thought anyone would rent Stone Bank. It's so isolated. But now that I've returned, and the cottage is occupied, Topper thinks this is a sign that he can come home.'

Topper flew on to the tall man's shoulder and sat on the mobile perch rubbing his tawny head against Daniel's chin. Nod, nod.

'He was homesick,' Daniel added, stroking the downy ruff of feathers.

'I've no time to play nursemaid to a homesick owl,' said Emma, busily collecting papers off the floor, her hair falling over her face. 'You'll have to make other arrangements.'

'That's a pity. I think Topper has taken to you. He can't live at the Lodge. My mother has cats.'

'Give him a good talking to,' said Emma. 'You might be able to reach a compromise. I really can't help.'

Daniel Masters paused on his way out. He seemed reluctant to go. 'By the way, if Lucinda phones, tell her I'm still climbing.'

Emma sat back on her heels. She had rented Stone Bank for peace and solitude and already she could expect a limping landlord calling, Lucinda telephoning and a two-legged shredding machine tap-dancing on her windowsill.

'This is a bit much,' she said. 'I've come down here to write a book but it seems I've got to pamper an owl and now take messages from your girlfriend.'

'Ex,' he said, disappearing.

She awoke next morning to the luxury of not having to go to the office. The hard set of Daniel's features immediately came into her mind. Had he a broken heart as well as a broken foot? Emma turned over; it was none of her business . . . was it?

Tap, tap. Topper asked politely to be allowed in. He had

emerged from a night's prowl in the woods and swooped down on to the window-ledge.

'Go away,' said Emma. 'Please.'

He flew on to the dressing table and discovered a box of face tissues. He shrieked with delight and began tearing them up, a mound of pink shreds growing round his feet.

Taking a beakful, he scuttled along the patchwork quilt and trampled tissues over the pillow. He wriggled himself into a hollow and lay his downy head next to Emma, blinking sleepily.

Emma was lost in enchantment. It was such a display of trust by a wild creature.

'OK, you can stay,' she said softly. 'But you've got to understand that my work is out of bounds.'

Nod, nod. Topper flopped over, content. In moments he was sleeping soundly.

As long as Emma provided Topper with plenty of scrap paper and string to tear up, he left her work alone. But he was a hoarder and stole pencils and hairclips and anything bright he fancied for a toy. He hid his treasures on a ledge above the curtains, along with mouldy crusts and cheese rinds he'd put away for a rainy day.

'How's the book getting on?' Daniel asked, stopping at the gate of Stone Bank Cottage and leaning on his stick.

Topper was sunbathing on the stone step, his three-foot wing span dazzling with iridescence from the sun's rays.

'It's not,' said Emma. 'I'm spending far too much time catching mice for Topper.'

'You're setting the traps like I showed you?'

'It's revolting. I prefer chopping up liver.'

She stroked the soft feathers between Topper's eyes. She

was no longer afraid of him. He had only once caught her fingers with his beak by accident. His beak was razor sharp and it made her realize how careful Topper was not to hurt her.

'Has Lucinda phoned?' Daniel never wasted words.

'Does it matter?' she said without thinking. 'You must have asked me a dozen times. She isn't going to phone. Why don't you give up?'

Emma bit her tongue with embarrassment. The imaginary Lucinda had been another intrusion on her work; willowy and elegant, the woman to match the man. Daniel's eyes lingered on her and Emma found herself caught up in his searching gaze.

'Is that what you think?'

'I'm sorry, I shouldn't have spoken that way,' said Emma. 'I don't know the circumstances. Forgive me, I should stick to knitting.'

'I can assure you that your knitting sounds far less complicated than my life at present,' he said drily.

He was gone before Emma could unravel those complications. She was none the wiser either. He was infuriating and fascinating. A man from the mountains.

She shook off a tidal wave of feeling. This was ridiculous, she told herself. Neither man nor owl could be allowed into her affections. She wished to be totally uninvolved.

As the weather improved, Emma worked in the garden collating chapters. She kept Topper out of mischief with some rags to tear up. But he was nipping at blades of grass, pausing to gaze at the fine azure sky and scudding clouds.

'What's calling to you?' she asked. 'Do you want to try your wings?'

The great dark eyes never left her, their full power turned

on. With a quickening of her heart, she realized why the bond between man and owl was so strong. They both longed and belonged to the wild. Topper longed for the topmost branch of the silver birch; Daniel's sights were set on the scary heights of an icy mountain. Lucinda did not stand a chance.

Topper began chittering with annoyance; it was an odd noise the owl made by clacking his tongue against the roof of his beak. He began bobbing about and swivelling his head, emitting furious squeaks and muffled shrieks.

'Whatever's the matter?' Emma was alarmed. She had never seen the little owl so angry and upset.

A woman was coming across the garden from the direction of the Lodge, Daniel at her side. She was wearing a silky suit, a wide-brimmed floppy hat shielding her Dresden skin from the sun.

'So this is your little pet owl, darling,' she said languidly. 'Isn't he sweet.' She held out a graceful hand, making appropriate bird-like noises. Daniel was a step behind her, his face a mask, but Emma knew this was Lucinda.

'What a dear baby thing,' she went on. 'You're always so original in everything you do. I suppose that's why we get on so well together. In every way,' she added for Emma's benefit.

Emma went cold with confusion. She made to gather her papers and disappear inside, when suddenly Topper took off. Silently and swiftly he flew straight at Lucinda's head, his razor-sharp talons held stiffly out in front of him. He was aiming for her face.

Just as swiftly, Emma reacted. She threw her heavy file at the owl; it caught him in full flight. He crash-landed on the grass. Furiously he turned his attack on Emma's notes, paper and feathers flying in all directions like a snowstorm.

Lucinda was clutching Daniel's arm, screaming, protecting her face against him.

'You're not hurt,' he said. 'I'll take you back to the Lodge. I don't think Topper likes you.'

'The beast, the beast,' she sobbed. 'The horrid little beast. I don't know why I came down here. I don't know why I bother with you at all.'

That evening Emma sat forlornly on the floor of the sitting room, surrounded by bits of paper, trying to salvage the work of years. Topper perched on the top of a lamp, looking faintly sheepish, if an owl can look sheepish, occasionally shaking his woolly head at the folly of humans.

'I am very cross with you,' said Emma. 'How could you be so naughty? You don't attack people just because they say silly things about you.'

Topper nodded and tap-tapped along the rim of the shade. He let out a rusty little whistle which was his way of saying sorry.

'I'm sorry, too,' said Daniel from the doorway. He was on his own. 'It was my fault for letting her come down. I should have known Topper wouldn't like her.' He held a pot of glue and a roll of Sellotape. 'Can I help with the first aid?'

His face had unfrozen, as if a great burden had been lifted. He had a devastating smile. Emma knew he would only be around until his foot healed, then he would be away. No one could hold him. Like Topper, he would go back to the wilds.

'I could do with some help. Topper made a good job of shredding my book.'

'Let's get started. We'll sort into piles by colour first;

then separate typing from photographs and patterns. Then I suggest each page is mounted on a sheet of paper, like a jigsaw. And as we go along you can tell me all about your book.'

'It'll take ages . . .'

'I've plenty of time.'

Emma returned his smile. Daniel would look good in a heavy-knit Whitby Guernsey. She knew just the right pattern, if she could find it, designed for the men of the Scottish fishing fleet. A size 44 chest? Ideal for mountaineering. Perhaps he would take it with him.

Topper emerged from a deep sleep just before dusk. She saw him gazing into the distant woods as if they were calling to him, telling him of the great outdoors waiting to be explored. With a powerful thrustback of his feet, he took off, his wings beating strongly, fast and true, as he sped towards the trees.

'He's gone,' she said, her voice catching. She watched him fly into the gathering darkness with tears in her eyes.

'Let him go and he'll come back,' said Daniel, close by her side. Was he telling her something? Emma hoped that he was. She hoped it would be true of both owl and man.

THE WITCH
OF WATFORD

It was not quite Watford but near enough. The woman they thought was a witch lived in a large village trying to expand into a small town with an annual consumption of meadows and green pastures. This rural carnage upset her but there was little she could do about it.

Elise wandered round the shops in long black clothes bought from the Oxfam shop, her raven hair flowing, her two cats following like little dogs. One was definitely black, as black as night, lean and sinewy; the other was a cheerfully striped tabby, a cushion-shaped creature . . . but, oh his eyes – they were as bright as chips of emerald glass.

'Sit,' she would say to the two cats outside the small grocer's shop. And the two cats sat obediently. But not for long. They got up, stretched, moved and sat inches away on better pitches of their own choice. When Elise returned with bags of clanking tins they greeted her with cries of delight as if she had been gone a year or more.

'My good pussies,' she would say, stroking each soft head in turn. 'My very good pussies. Let's go home now.'

And they would turn, knowing the way without bidding. They followed her back to their cottage, ignoring the leers of lazy dogs. Some people thought that the tumbledown dwelling moved, shifted nearer the trees, then away, but they couldn't be sure. It had once been an old forge; the furnace was still there, cold now. But sometimes in the night people fancied they saw the flicker and glow of a fire. It was strange when the furnace had been cold for years.

The villagers were always talking about Elise and her two cats, and the shifting cottage and the glowing fire. They also talked about her shopping habits.

'Cat food, cat treats, cat biscuits.'

'Coley and fish heads.'

'Melts and lights.'

'But what does she eat? Sometimes she buys an orange.'

The shopkeepers shook their heads. The wives nodded their heads. Perhaps Elise did not need ordinary food or maybe she cast a spell on the coley and it became smoked salmon.

They noticed something else mysterious. She disappeared for days on end. And so did the two cats. They all vanished and the cottage was empty, sometimes shifting a few yards this way or that. Now it was standing nearer the path. And the flowers were blooming when all other gardens had long settled into their winter sleep. Her flowers bloomed at the oddest times: daffodils in autumn, tulips in winter. She never cut the lawn. The weeds only came up at night and were withered by morning.

The two cats said nothing although they understood what was being thought. They knew everything. They knew that Elise had a very serious problem and she was not concentrating on her calling. Twice she had forgotten to stop the grass growing and in the morning they'd had to leap over stalks a foot high and a forest of nettles.

The cats sat and looked at each other. How could they help her? They chewed thoughtfully on shreds of grass and glared at the sparrows twittering rudely in the trees above. It was a day for action but without Elise they were more or less devitalized.

Elise sat before her mirror painting on black eyeliner and putting on nine of her collection of silver rings. She always wore nine. It was a significant number in her life. She looked like a black witch, but she was actually a white witch. There was not a malevolent bone in her body. In fact, she was incurably romantic but being a witch was definitely a drawback when it came to finding someone to love.

She made her living selling love potions at fairgrounds around the country. Each potion was concocted and mixed individually. The lovelorn consulted her and after considering all aspects of the relationship, including obscure points such as the shape of nose and length of fingers, Elise would produce the right love potion for the right couple. It took a deal of thought and skill. Witchcraft had nothing to do with it.

While she was away, the cats disappeared into the woods.

Clients came and clients went, most of them thoroughly satisfied with the love potion prescribed. A high proportion of them were successful and grateful cards of thanks and wedding invitations arrived at her cottage. The postmen liked delivering the mail to her. It was never raining along her path.

'If my potion doesn't work, then it's not the fault of the potion,' she always told her clients. 'The relationship is not right. It is not meant to be and, believe me, you are better off apart.'

No one could argue with that.

She had been nine years old when she discovered she was a witch. It was not a frivolous discovery but a deeply moving experience. A cat told her. She had found the cat sprawled in the gutter, injured by a car. Her tears fell on the helpless animal. She did not know what to do. As she stroked the muddied brown fur her tears turned to crystal and the cat stirred in her arms.

The small pounding heart steadied and rallied. Elise's hands felt a warmth spreading to the cat, healing waves that rippled through his body. She lowered her head and breathed on him and her breath showered him with a fine sparkling dust.

The cat nudged Elise's ear with a damp nose. She could not believe her thoughts. It was as if the cat were speaking to her and she was understanding every word.

Nine days later her hair turned raven black. Her mother did not seem to notice. That was very strange. Perhaps she had clouded her mother's eyes so that she would not be disturbed by the change in her daughter.

Nine months later Elise was in class at school when she rose an inch off the floor. She thought it was something to do with the history lesson on Ancient Greeks which was one hundred per cent boring. It was a strange feeling. She spent the rest of the period going up and down like a yo-yo till she was dizzy. It was not something she did often, only when she was bored rigid.

Then she found she could move things, small things at first, like spoons or the cruet on the table. It puzzled her parents when they reached for a fork only to find it had shifted. She grew out of moving things and just moved the cottage. She did it for a change of view or to catch the sun. She needed warmth desperately. That's why she wore so many layers of clothes and lit the furnace on cold nights.

The cats tried to keep her warm at night, one stretched on either side, but it wasn't enough. The heat from their bodies only unfroze a small part of her. It was as if she stored her healing powers in a mental deep-freeze and the electricity for it was generated from her body heat. Sometimes she saw icicles fall from her limbs. Her metabolism was so slow that she rarely needed to eat.

Elise's problem began at a convention for healers. All sorts of people were there including reflexologists and aromatherapists. Unknown to Elise there was also a camera crew from a regional TV station which wanted a light item to round off an evening news bulletin. A haven of healers seemed to fit the bill.

Elise got stuck with a very boring young man who was mesmerized by her long dark hair. He rabbited on about his various auras and multidimensional experiences and Elise switched off. She was a practical, down-to-earth witch and was not comfortable with things she did not understand. Just when she thought her legs would buckle with boredom, she saw a man elbowing his way towards her through the crowd. She knew he was coming to see her because her name was written across his forehead.

'Would you excuse us?' he said, shouldering the boring

one out of the way. He turned to Elise. 'I'm Mark E. Redford, the producer with this motley crew. Could you do that again for us please? We didn't quite catch it.'

'Do what again?' she said faintly.

'Go up to the ceiling.'

The cats knew that something had gone desperately wrong at the convention when Elise called them in from the woods that evening. She gave them an orange for their supper and moved the cottage twice in the space of an hour. They looked at each other with enigmatic expressions that spoke volumes.

'I've fallen in love,' she told them, scooping up armfuls of wriggling fur and legs and paws on to her lap. 'With a human being. And a television producer of all people. No potion, no charms, not even a pinch of comfrey. The trouble is he's not the slightest bit interested in me as a woman. He's only interested in getting me to do tricks for his stupid programmes. Of course, I refused. But it's only made him more determined. His name is Mark E. Redford. Oh dear . . .' she wailed. 'That's the first three letters of Merlin . . .'

The cats ran their claws through the tangle of her hair and nudged her face. They both noticed she was warmer. She did not light the furnace that night, but stayed up late mixing a very particular potion.

'Ginger for travel, marigolds for control . . . no, no . . . I don't want to control him. His eyes are grey so midnight water from the spring and some old purple foxgloves for stimulation. Of course, mountain ash is pretty good but it's so greedy. Seeds from the laurel to keep him safe . . . and cloves from Persia for desire.'

Mark Redford, without his crew, arrived on the doorstep

of the cottage the next morning. He looked with amazement at the profusion of cherry blossom and the drift of pink petals floating down to the grass when not a breath of air stirred. Elise had felt like cherry blossom when she awoke and had encouraged the sap to rise.

Still she was surprised when she saw Mark on her door-step and almost moved the cottage to cover her embarrassment. It must have been the ginger fumes working at a distance.

'Don't worry, Elise,' he said swiftly. 'I've come alone. No nasty cameras lurking in the bushes. I say, isn't your cherry blossom a bit early?'

'No, it's ten o'clock,' she said, wrapping herself in another black shawl. 'Come in and I'll make some dandelion coffee.' She thought of her potion which had stood overnight in a crystal goblet and was ready.

'Nice cats,' he said as the animals inspected his shoes and politely sniffed the hem of his jeans. 'What are they called?'

'I don't know. They haven't told me. I don't know who they were.'

'Who they were?'

'In another life.'

'Your cats talk to you?' he said without a flicker of surprise.

'Yes.' It was Elise who looked surprised. 'Don't all cats?'

He ran his hand through his untidy brown hair. 'Come to think of it, I suppose my mother's cat is rather vocal.'

'You haven't been listening properly,' said Elise, nodding to her cats.

The cats took themselves away a few feet to watch the couple drinking coffee in the garden. They liked this tall, funny human who was the first three letters of Merlin and, if Elise played her cards right, she could have children called Lana, Iain and Norc. They judged Mark to be exactly right for her and already in his heart he was fascinated by what he saw. And the dandelion coffee didn't taste too bad. But at the same time he was scared of her unusual powers. They sat in the garden talking for hours. When Elise moved the cottage to catch the last of the autumn sunshine, Mark almost leaped into his car and drove off at speed. His hand shook slightly.

'I ought to be going,' he said, exit written all over his forehead. 'I've a programme to make.'

'You'll have a good journey,' she said. 'There are no traffic hold-ups.'

And there weren't. Which surprised him on that stretch of the motorway.

Elise called at the Oxfam shop and went mad. She bought lots of black clothes, a silk blouse, a swirling embroidered skirt, a lacy scarf as fine as a cobweb. It was the nearest she had ever got to being extravagant.

Mark came again. He could not keep away but the apprehension was always there that she might turn him into a six-foot toad. Elise knew this and grew increasingly unhappy till she could stand it no longer and moved the entire cottage into the middle of the wood.

The cats stared at each other in dismay. Did this mean the end of all that scrummy shop cat food? Had they got to catch their own supper in future? But what could they do? They knew a few odd spells but nothing particularly helpful. They could appear and disappear without anyone noticing. They could slip back into the past for a quick reconnoitre, their whiskers twitching as they relived long lost experiences and wondered at the complexity of human evolution.

'What am I going to do?' asked Elise, burying her head in the softness of their tummies. 'Mark doesn't trust me. He's afraid of what I might do.'

They jumped away from her. She was covering them in wetness from her eyes. They had never seen her cry before. Witches didn't cry. This was more than ordinarily serious. It was a catastrophe.

The two cats picked up the sound of his car coming from a long way off, even before he had turned into the lane. They went to meet him, their plan as yet unformed, but they agreed silently they had to do something.

It was one of their days for not touching the ground so they walked along the top of the fence, then leaped from branch to branch, waiting for him at the turn of the lane. As his car drove into sight they both hurled themselves at the windscreen like catapults. The car swerved, hit a hedge, slithered sideways off the road and turned over with a sickening screech into the ditch. Its wheels spun furiously.

The cats sat back, appalled at the damage they had caused; they began to groom their ruffled fur as if they were only passing spectators. Elise had heard the noise of screeching brakes and ran bare-foot out of the woods. Mark was slumped against the steering wheel, blood oozing from his forehead. Nothing was written on it at all.

Elise did not hesitate. She moved the car on to the road, the right way up. By the time she had got Mark out of the driving seat, he was beginning to stir and moan.

'Please don't die,' she whispered, tenderly wiping away the blood with leaves of mint. 'I love you so much. I've got all the right herbs for this cut – comfrey, which is basic for cell repair, calendula, which is antiseptic and anti-inflammatory, St John's Wort for the pain, lavender oil for calming. There won't even be a scar, my darling.'

She moved the cottage back to its original site, only just in the nick of time. In fact it was so close one of the chimneys got left behind. Her hair gradually changed to a soft shade of brown and she grew so warm she had to shed her shawls and long skirts. The weeds began a last spurt of growing and the cherry blossom tree faded to a wintery gauntness.

'Elise, what has happened?' Mark groaned. 'I came to tell you that I can't live without you. I don't care if you are a witch.'

She laughed delightedly. 'Whatever made you think I was a witch?' she said, her eyes sparkling. 'You've been watching too much television.'

Afterwards Elise often wondered what had really happened but she couldn't remember. The cats knew. It had been the ninth day of the ninth month. And she had spoken openly of her love for a human. It was simply impossible for her to remain a witch in such circumstances.

The cats sat and waited patiently. They were pinning their hopes on little Lana.

LEAVE OF ABSENCE
(True Story)

She did not come in for supper but I hardly gave it a thought. She was often late, preferring to eat alone and in dignity without three athletic kittens leap-frogging over her, or the kittens' young mother patting her nose or big red Rufus stealing the best bits off her dish.

Every half an hour I called her, front door and garden door.

'Clover, Clover.'

It was raining a steady drizzle and her long dark tortoiseshell coat would be getting soaked. Each time I half expected her to slide in like an otter. She was so dark she could merge with the shadows and often I'd find she'd come in between my feet whilst I was still calling.

The evening drew on with typing and television and

kittens and calling Clover, and the garden shrank within walls of darkness. Somewhere out there in the hostile night was Clover, refusing to hear me, shutting her ears against my calls, turning her haughty nose the other way.

I suppose the three kittens arriving all at once with their young nursing mother, still only nine months old herself, were too much for Clover to take. Their arrival was unannounced, like refugees arriving on the doorstep. With one ill-considered phone call I changed her life. And she already had a lot to put up with from Rufus, who demanded to be first in everything, letting in, letting out, and growled at her if she dare put her small Persian nose one centimetre ahead of his. She knew her place. She crouched back, dark and submissive, like an arab slave girl or a teeny-weeny Victorian maidservant, allowing the lion-headed Sultan, master of the household, his rightful domination.

The arrival of the kittens, miniature mewing scraps crawling about the floor, must have been a shock. And their mother, a thin scrawny single parent, thrown out by panicking owners. Suddenly the newcomers were crowding Clover's kitchen, all over the place with their big pen and bedding box. A litter tray from the past appeared. Clover and Rufus sat and stared at the intruders, shattered.

They both hissed, politely, repeatedly. Everybody made a lot of fuss of the big cats. It was not that Clover and Rufus were ignored because of the new, helpless family. Quite the reverse. They got extra cuddles, treats and stroking. Clover's spine stiffened in my arms. She was not so easily taken in.

Rufus succumbed. He became the adored uncle, washing the kittens, temporary pillow for tired little baby bodies. He approved of the nursing mother's eight meals a day and stood in line for his. He put on weight.

Clover watched his capitulation with derision. Where was all that male dominance now? One flighty little silver teen-age mum, now quiet and docile, and he was putty in her paws.

As the kittens grew bigger and more agile, new tactics were required. Feeding all six at once was like trying to curb a stampede of wild buffalo with a feather, though the adult cats sat back with patience while I chopped and delivered. The kittens were not so well behaved. They jumped up, ran along working tops, clawed, fought, stole food from right under my fork. It gave me a headache.

We developed sittings. Three at a time. Three adult cats at a time if it worked out that way. We got devious at putting the kittens out for a run round the garden just before a meal. Sometimes Clover fed alone and that was ideal. Her full-throated purr said how much she appreciated civilized eating. Her mat has apple blossom on it.

That morning she'd had to breakfast with the entire mob, her place at the end of the row as usual but still with maraud-ing kittens raiding any food in sight. All that pushing and shoving and stealing must have been very disconcerting. She asked to go out almost immediately without even waiting to see if there were second helpings.

I did not see her all day which was unusual. She usually sauntered in looking for a soft bed for a snooze.

Not a sign of her at suppertime. I began to get vague flutters of apprehension.

By midnight I was out in the garden in the rain, nightdress clinging round my ankles, calling and calling, rattling the biscuit tin, flashing a lamp. She had a sweet tooth and loved biscuits. No wet fur came to anoint my feet; no sharp claws snagged my dressing gown, no cold nose purred into my ear.

Front door, garden door. It went on for an hour. Go to bed, I told myself. She's caught a squirrel and is sleeping it off in some warm hollow. She's playing hard to get. She's got shut in someone's garage or garden shed. She's left home and gone to live a pampered life with a rich family two roads away. The cat robbers have taken her for her long fur to make into a hat. She's been run over and is groaning in a gutter. A fox has got her.

The bed was friendless, empty, with no noisy forty-minute bedtime washing and chomping going on at my feet. No long body stretched out widthways while I cling to the edge. No clawing or pounding into the softness of my stomach, claws penetrating the duvet.

Nothing.

She had gone.

I dreamed of her. I dreamed I found her in the meadow among the grass, bloodied and mauled, unable to move. I took off my sweater and lifted her on to it; carried her swiftly to the vet's in my arms. I ran into the vet's surgery in my vest. 'Please, please,' I pleaded at the counter. 'My cat's been mauled. You must help her.' The vet had a big needle. 'I must put her out so that I can examine her,' he said. 'Don't do it. Don't inject her. Give her a chance,' I wept, thinking he meant the final needle, kneeling on the floor, my face level with hers.

Her large amber eyes asked for another chance.

I awoke, knowing instantly that today I had to start look-ing for her. Twenty-four hours was enough. I would search the meadows at the end of the garden. I would call at neigh-bours' and ask them to look in locked sheds. I would put a photo of Clover (she is so beautiful) on the gate and a notice. Take photos and notices into all the villages. Phone the police.

My heart sank at all that had to be done. I must find her. If she was lost, I knew I would never forgive myself. I would always bear the guilt.

A small, dark, splodged face peered round the edge of the door then leaped on to my bed. She was wet, bedraggled, burrs stuck all over the damp and spiky stomach fur. She trampled over my bed leaving a satisfactory trail of dirt and leaves.

'Clover! Clover!' I buried my face in her fur, too relieved to speak. 'Where on earth have you been?'

She curled herself round and round, and round again into a damp ball by my side. She glanced at me, momentarily, smugly.

She has slept on my bed all day, the sleep of the exhausted. I creep up to look at her every few hours, like an anxious mother. Where had she been? Had she walked miles through the tangled undergrowth of the rain-lashed Chart, then changed her mind and walked back? Had she sat, still and watchful, at a distance from the house, waiting to see if a crateful of kittens was carted out?

I kneel by the bed and rub my face in the soft fur of her head, remembering that dream. Now I recognize those eyes that pleaded with me for a second chance. They were mine.

THE GLASS CAT

Sometimes the glass cat was there and sometimes it appeared not to be. It depended on the light, the weather and what was behind it. That's why they called it the glass cat. It had no other name. Rain was always visible. A faint diagonal haze that never permeated the fur but shrouded the cat in mist.

No one knew how long the cat had been in the house. One said a year, one said yesterday, another, nearer the mark, said it arrived the day they moved in. The family argued about it automatically. They always argued. It was a family trait, a sort of verbal bonding.

The person who argued the least was the daughter, Nancy. She was adopted, a slight, remote girl, somewhat like the cat which appeared from nowhere. Her mind was quiet and she rarely opened her mouth. But this quietness had been forced on her.

'That damned cat ruined my new shirt yesterday,' said Reg, the son, who didn't like the animal's unequivocal stare.

Nancy raised an eyebrow. She did not believe him. She had dark eloquent eyebrows and cornflower blue eyes. Her skin was as translucent as a painting by Renoir but an infection in childhood had damaged her vocal chords. She was told not to speak for six months. When the time was over, it seemed simpler not to speak at all. She hadn't spoken for years.

'Nancy!' It was a stern reprimand. 'Now then, we don't want any of those looks. That girl can speak volumes when she wants to.'

Nancy flinched. So did the glass cat. Nancy was not sure if the cat was deaf. Sometimes it did not seem to hear the family arguing. Yet she was told the whole road could hear their raised voices.

Nancy held the cat up to her face, brushing the fur against her cheek like a swan's-down puff, taking comfort from the gentleness of the velvet paws padding and kneading. The cat trampled through her hair, braiding the strands, growling a low decibel of contentment. Nancy saw a rainbow through him and then realized it was the colour of the striped curtains transmitted through his fur.

'Do I have to do all the work around here?' Mrs Burrows was yelling from the kitchen. Her husband was lounging in a green chair in a green pullover like a surfeit of frog's spawn. 'Am I the only person who can make a cup of tea? This is the kettle. This is the teapot. This is the milk.' She banged the objects down on the table with percussion-like precision.

Nancy winced and held the cat closer.

'Call this tea?' Mr Burrows retaliated. 'Second-grade dishwater would go down better. Been recycling the tea-bags again?'

'When do we eat?' asked Reg, not even looking up from his body-building magazine. 'Do we always have to wait? I'm starving.'

'Wait? Wait? Who's waiting? I'm not. I know where the food is kept even if you don't.'

'So I have to know where it's kept to get anything to eat. Is that a new rule then? Have you got a copy of the rules? I'd like to see them in writing.'

'Learned to read now, have we? That's a turn-up. Better tell the neighbours. Put up posters. Get a newsflash on the local radio.'

Nancy shuddered and her body turned to ice. She was going to have to leave home, if she could call this madhouse a home. She could not stand it. But where and when? And could she take the glass cat with her?

'Oh, cat,' she thought into his pearly ear. 'What am I going to do? There must be some way to escape.'

The cat was dark at night. He absorbed the darkness into his fur and became one of night's shadows. He lay waiting for Nancy as she returned from her evening class. No one went to meet her. They were all too busy. Mr Burrows was busy critically analysing the television; Mrs Burrows was critically analysing the critical analysis. Reg was busy body-building his body in his room with tape, video and mirrors.

Nancy was learning shorthand and typing at evening class. She was not sure how she was going to do it but she had decided to type her way to freedom. It had become a burning resolution. In her mind her typing speed was related to her speed of departure.

As she opened the front gate the cat came out of the shadows and twisted himself round her ankles like a sinewy rope. He had no beginning and no end. He was continuous cat.

'Shut that door!' Three Burrows voices shouted above the screeching of a car chase on television.

'She has shut it.'

'What's that draught then? A sandstorm from the Sahara?'

Nancy stood in the doorway, bewildered by the onslaught. She had shut the door. Yet a wind blew through the hall, disturbing the dried flowers on the wall.

She made herself a hot drink, then crept up to her room with her books and the glass cat. She would spend an hour practising her shorthand outlines. She could do sixty words a minute now. Why was the outline for cat so small? The glass cat curled up on the windowsill and vanished against the woodwork but she could hear his breathing, the lightest rush of air, like tiny wings. He was painfully endearing even when she could not see him. She would never be able to leave him behind, but how could she ever cope in a bed-sit with a job and a cat and limited means of communication? It would be impossible.

'I need a fairy godmother, like Cinderella,' she confided to the night sky, picking out the brightest star as the focus of her thoughts. 'Not necessarily the coach and gown bit, and you can keep the handsome prince, just some means of escape.'

The glass cat stretched himself as she slept and the moonlight flooded through him, turning his fur to silver. He had heard all she had ever thought to him, every word of every sentence. He could have gone long ago but he stayed for her sake. Many times the wind had offered to take him away. The rain, too, coruscating all those crystal droplets. But particularly the friendly darkness. The night was continually tempting him with release, drawing him into her shadows, showing him a glorious, untasted freedom.

But he could not go yet. She alone loved him when the others shouted; let him in when they kicked him out; cuddled him when they ignored him for days.

The family arguing only came a close second to the family television. They watched everything: repeats of repeats; all the game shows: they adored the advertisements. The adverts were as familiar as their own faces.

'It's Beattie!' they shrieked to each other. 'Come and see Beattie. The Gold Blend girl! Look, she's done her hair different. Ah, that lovely puppy . . .'

Nancy worked on in her room, letting the glass cat trample over her books and her papers. The cat loved sitting on whatever was holding her attention. He sat on newspapers, books, knitting, sewing, ironing like a glass paperweight.

The teacher at the evening class told Nancy she was nearly ready to look for a job.

'Of course,' he said carefully, 'it may be a little difficult to find exactly the right sort of work for you.'

She nodded, turning away so that the careful teacher would not see the despair in her eyes.

Yesterday's newspaper lay unread on the floor of her room. The glass cat was curled upon it, so pale, so glistening, that Nancy could almost read the print through his fur. She sat down beside him, absent-mindedly stroking the gossamer coat, her glance on the print. She read the advertisement twice before its significance sank in. A small charity for the deaf and dumb needed a junior secretary, someone who would be willing to learn sign language as the staff were without hearing.

Her breath came in big gasps. She could do this. Even if she did not speak, she could be their ears, then type or sign the words. She cut out the advertisement and began to write a letter to them.

The day that Nancy moved out, the glass cat vanished. He went on a dull day when it rained rods of water; he went like smoke, fog, a wraith of mist. He simply disappeared into the rain. Nancy was sad but she knew she could not deny him his freedom, especially when she had gained hers.

As she unpacked a crate in the tiny flat over the charity's offices in London, her hand closed on a smooth, round object. Nancy opened her hand and in it lay a small glass cat, curled for ever in crystal sleep, its nose tucked into a long tail. A noise came from her throat. A gasp of recognition. A sound which would one day become a word. She held the ornament against her cheek and the strange thing was, the glass cat was not cold. It was warm.

PORCUPINE BABY
(True Story)

They called the pretty female cat Doodle-bug. It was the oddest name but she had survived a doodle-bug raid in the Second World War and was found among the smouldering ruins of a demolished house in Romford. A family took pity on the cat and gave her a home.

'She'll have to be called Doodle-bug,' they said.

At the end of the war, about the same time as Doodle-bug had her first litter of three kittens, both the father and sixteen-year-old son lost their jobs. The economic situation was depressed and work was hard to find. There were eight mouths to feed ... two adults, two children, one cat and three kittens.

But the mother was not a woman to sit at home, wringing her hands with despair. If there was no work for the menfolk, then she would find employment. She searched for weeks while the family grew hungry.

Then work arrived at their home in the form of a huge stack of sheets of brown paper and a large amber lump. It was solid glue. This was the raw material for making paper carrier bags for a stall in Romford market.

'This is our work,' said the mother to her open-mouthed family. 'We are going to turn ourselves into a production line making carrier bags.'

Doodle-bug rolled over so that her greedy kittens could feed. At least she did not have to work.

It was slave labour. Everyone had to help. The mother explained the method. A fold was made along the top, then the sheet was folded in half and glued along the side seam. The bottom quarter was folded up, then began the complicated cross-folding that formed the gusset of the carrier bag. The gusset was the difficult part, rather like making a paper dart without wings. Soon they could do it in their sleep.

Doodle-bug and her kittens watched this kitchen industry with curiosity. They were not allowed to play with the paper, mustn't touch the glue. Every sheet represented money, and one wasted was a small calamity. The cats watched the melting down of the lump of glue in a big pot, wondering if this revolting smell of fish bones was their supper. They hoped not. Doodle-bug was still feeding her kittens and was always ravenously hungry. She waited patiently, dreaming of food.

'Urgh, what a dreadful smell,' said the small, tousle-haired daughter, wrinkling her nose. 'Whatever is it made of?'

'I don't dare think,' said her mother, stirring the big pot.

She had practically sprained her wrists, breaking up the lump of glue with a hammer, melting it down with water until it was liquid. It was an unpleasant chore but she had to do it.

'Off you go to bed, Marion. We'll leave it to cool overnight.'

She lifted the heavy pot carefully on to the floor. Steam clung to her face and hair. She brushed away the wet strands wearily. The glue would be cool by the morning and then they could start work, glueing the next batch of bags.

It had been a long day and she was tired, but she found time to give Doodle-bug a saucer of milk and stroke the fat, sleepy kittens nuzzling against their mother. She planned to start work before breakfast. Marion would help. She was a good girl and had nimble fingers.

The grey and white kitten was the smallest and liveliest of the litter. She never kept still, always wriggling and dancing around. She opened one cornflower blue eye, twitching her tiny pink nose at the fishy smell. She was not altogether sure if it was delicious or not. But she was going to have a look.

She scampered along the floor, tail high, ears perked, whiskers trembling with excitement. She sniffed at the pot, wondering how to find out what was inside.

The family were in the parlour. There was no television in those days. The father was reading the penny paper. The son was playing cards. Marion was getting ready for bed, scrubbed and polished in clean pyjamas. It was a quiet evening, no sirens. So no one was prepared for the howl that suddenly erupted from the kitchen, an eerie sound that sent prickles skittering down their spines.

'Whatever's that?'

'It's coming from the kitchen.'

'Hurry . . . something's happened.'

They all rushed into the kitchen, scared of what they might find. The howls grew louder.

Doodle-bug was standing with her front paws gripping the rim of the glue pot, crying in terrible distress, her mouth wide open, her eyes stark with fear. The smallest kitten was in the pot of glue submerged up to its neck, floundering around helplessly on its back. It was squeaking pitifully.

The woman did not hesitate. She scooped the kitten out of the hot liquid and plonked it in the kitchen sink, turning on the water tap. Her hands smarted with pain, skin turning red.

'Oh, my goodness, how are we going to get this glue off you,' she said, rolling up her sleeves despite the pain. 'It's bath-time for you, little baby. Now stop howling, Doodle, your kitten is safe.'

Marion lifted the mother cat so that she could see the kitten cowering in the sink. 'There's your kitten,' she said.

She ran to get the soap flakes. Both soap and soap flakes were rationed and precious but this was an emergency. She stood on tiptoe at the sink, helping to splash water on the sticky kitten and calm its trembling.

The kitten was too petrified to struggle. It could hardly move, paws and fur gummed into a sodden mess. The blue eyes were wide with fright, tiny pink mouth opening and squeaking like a bird.

'Good thing it didn't go in head first,' said the mother. 'She doesn't seem to have swallowed any and she's breathing all right.'

The kitten had several baths in lukewarm water, followed by rinses. Its thick fur had saved it from scalding. The kitchen sink became a nasty sticky mess of glue and fur, the water swirling around in a grey morass.

Marion sniffed at her wrinkled fingers and wet pyjamas. 'I hope I don't smell like this for school tomorrow. I'll get teased.'

'You just tell them that you rescued your kitten from a pot of glue,' said her mother. 'That'll shut them up.'

'My kitten?' Marion hesitated. 'Can I keep the kitten then? Mummy . . . ?'

She had been wanting the smallest kitten but did not dare say so. She knew money was tight and there were already enough mouths to feed. It must have been a slip of the tongue. She patted the kitten gently with a towel and set it down near its mother. It wobbled towards her maternal warmth on matchstick legs, shaking them, its tail dragging wetly on the floor.

'We'll see. Leave it to sleep now, get over the shock. Come along, my girl. It's bedtime for you, too.'

The kitten spent the night close to its mother, its fur drying in the warm circle of her body. It was exhausted by the terrifying ordeal, the waterfall of water from the tap, the huge splashes, the soap bubbles rising up in the sink like a swamp . . .

The family got up for breakfast, talking about the rescue and first-aid operation, the mother making little of her scalded hand. Doodle-bug was suckling her kittens in the corner of the kitchen. Marion went on her knees and stroked the fat, contented little bodies squirming and kneading with a chorus of purring.

'Mum! There's only two. The smallest one has gone!'

The glue pot had been covered over for the night and there was no way the kitten could have climbed back in.

They searched everywhere, under the table, in cupboards, behind the dresser.

In the darkest corner of the kitchen they found the kitten. It was shivering miserably. The kitten's fur had dried into stiff needle-sharp spikes like a porcupine, and her mother had rejected her, driven her away from the tender teats on her stomach.

'I'm not surprised,' said mother. 'Those spikes look pretty painful. And I thought we'd got it all out.'

She lifted out the kitten. Its coat was practically solid with dried glue. It was pretty strong stuff.

'What can we do for Spiky?' Marion looked at her mother, fearing that there might be nothing more. Her eyes filled with tears. She knew her mother had more than enough to do. Housework and shopping and cooking and all those wretched carrier bags to fold and glue. The mother sighed. And here was her small daughter asking for more . . . for the sake of a half-dead kitten.

'Fetch my hair shampoo,' she said briskly. 'It's back to the sink.'

For the next three days operation-shampoo was top of their priorities. The kitten was continually shampooed in the sink, fed milk through a dropper, washed again. They lost count of the number of times. The precious shampoo liquid disappeared. Each shampoo removed a little more of the awful stuff and they had to handle the tiny kitten very carefully. Somehow meals were fitted in and carrier bags folded.

At last every vestige of glue was rinsed from its fur and it dried to a normal baby softness. Doodle-bug took the squeaky-clean kitten back into the fold after a few suspicious sniffs.

Spiky bore all the ablutions without complaint or struggle, knowing in some way that it had to be done.

They gave the other two kittens away. There was no way that Spiky could leave the family after such an adventure.

'We're stuck with her,' said the son.

She grew into a beautiful grey and white tabby cat with an elegant plume for a tail. She had a loving nature, as if she knew they had saved her life. She eventually had kittens of her own.

But she never forgot those three days of non-stop baths. She developed a total aversion to water and never went anywhere near it. She would not drink it. She refused to go out in the rain. She always took a wide detour down the side of the garden to avoid the goldfish pond.

The days of the carrier bag kitchen industry passed and fortunes changed. Marion became a well-known writer of children's stories, the porcupine baby a loving childhood memory.

PRICKLY LADY

The other half of the house had been empty for more than
a year. Jules did not mind the blank windows and unswept
path, but the tangled brambles, overgrown weeds and grass
were a challenge he could not ignore. He had taken to
trespassing in the nicest possible way, mowing the neglected
lawn a little here, trimming the dividing hedge a little there.
It became difficult to see where one garden began and the
other ended as edges blurred and plants spread.

But his life was divided into a pattern that verged on the
sublime and the ridiculous. He spent four frantic days in
London working impossibly long hours as a city stockbroker; then sped towards the green belt for a long weekend
of unwinding, gardening and reading in his semi-detached
slate and stone cottage.

When a 'SOLD' sign suddenly appeared on the other half he was resentful and disturbed. He liked having both gardens to tend. He liked the peace and quiet. He did not want a neighbour.

He was mildly curious about the new owner, but no one down at The Spotted Dog seemed to know anything.

'I did hear it were someone who had summit to do with Dallas,' said Old Jim through clouds of pipe smoke from his corner by the fire.

'Dallas?'

'That there telly programme with Joanie Collick.'

'Joan Collins? Dynasty?'

'That's what I said,' said Old Jim, coughing.

Jules was no wiser when he climbed into his two-seater sports car for the drive back to the cottage. He would be polite but distant. He would make it clear from the start that he liked privacy and was not the sort to lend a cup of sugar.

The road to the isolated cottages was long and winding so he dropped his speed to a steady twenty. Even so he was not prepared, on taking a particularly blind corner, to find another car stationary in the middle of the tarmac.

He crashed on his brakes and stopped inches from the other car's bumper and red rear lights. He leaned out of the window.

'What the hell are you doing?' he shouted angrily.

'Sorry,' a voice floated back. 'Pedestrian crossing.'

Jules peered into the headlights and darkness beyond. But he could see no one. He revved the engine impatiently, waiting for the car ahead to move. He hit the horn.

'Still crossing,' the voice continued, disembodied.

Eventually, with much grinding of gears and labouring

of engine, the other car started up. Now Jules could see that it was an ancient Morris, a model long gone to the scrapheaps. There seemed to be no way of overtaking and he resigned himself to following it all the way home.

An owl hooted in the eerie darkness and in that split second of inattention the old heap ahead stopped again and Jules had to slam on his brakes for a second time. He wrenched open his door and swung out his long legs. He was going to give that dozy driver a piece of his mind.

At the same moment, the other driver's door opened and into Jules's headlights stepped a vision in primrose. The unfastened lapels of the wide-shouldered loose jacket revealed a pale satiny dress. Bobbed cornsilk hair swung in the breeze. Jules glimpsed slim legs in absurdly high-heels disappearing round the front of the car.

'Dallas,' Jules said under his breath. 'Excuse me,' he said aloud, striding after her. 'Is this some kind of game?'

'Would you keep your voice down? It's scared enough as it is. They've got very sensitive hearing.'

'What have?'

'Hedgehogs. They're nearly blind, you know, but make up for it with their hearing and sense of smell.'

Jules couldn't believe it. 'You're not trying to tell me that twice I have endangered life and limb, not to mention my expensive car, for . . . a hedgehog?'

She turned a pair of incredibly steely-blue eyes on him. 'Could you live with a squashed hedgehog on your conscience?' she asked in tones of ice.

'Easily,' he said.

'Monster,' she said. 'How would you like a road built right across the path you've always used to get to a favourite bush or hedge?'

'This road has been here years even if it was only resurfaced last spring. You're not trying to tell me that this, er . . . hedgehog remembers when it was a path?'

'It's probably in the genes. Hereditary memory. These little creatures have been around for twenty million years.'

'Has the little creature crossed the road yet?' Jules asked with barely contained contempt. 'I would like to get home before dawn.'

'This one's frozen up instead of running. It's their natural defence. Look, it's rolled into a ball.'

Jules peered on the ground. A small dark mound lay on the tarmac a few feet from the car wheels. He was momentarily touched by its defencelessness.

'Perhaps if we went carefully, we could drive either side of it?'

She shot him a scathing glance and reached into her car. She brought out a square scarf. With infinite care she covered the prickles and carried the hedgehog to the safety of the thick hedge.

'There you go,' she said softly. She turned to Jules. 'Sorry to have kept you from wherever you were going.'

'Just a party,' he shrugged. 'An all-nighter.'

'I thought you said you were going home,' she said, coaxing the old engine into noisy life and driving off.

Jules awoke late the next morning, a foreign sound splitting the country air and blasting his ears. He staggered to the window, draped in a duvet, rubbing his eyes. The Dallas lady was up a ladder, cleaning windows, a small transistor on the windowsill broadcasting weather forecasts, the top ten, news bulletins to the world. Jules groaned. He had guessed right. She was his new neighbour. His peaceful way of life could vanish . . .

She was tall and slim in blue jeans and a baggy shirt, a sweatband keeping her hair from her face. Jules took in her appearance without the slightest degree of pleasure.

She caught sight of Jules pointing to her transistor, his jaw shadowed and grim, dark hair tousled.

'Recognized your car in the carport,' she said, turning down the volume. 'Was it a nice party?'

'Smashing,' he said, knowing that she must have heard his arrival time, even though he had driven around for a while. 'I'm Jules Brandon. Apparently we're neighbours.'

'Ursula Sloane. Sissy to my friends.'

'Sloane? Is that a name? Isn't it a green wellie?'

She ignored the slur and waved an arm towards her efficiently shorn lawn. 'Much as I appreciate your neighbourliness,' she began, 'I do not want my lawn cut or my hedge trimmed. I am not into the suburban scene. So would you kindly keep your mower and your trimmer to yourself.'

'Going to pave it over with concrete?' asked Jules, smarting. 'I believe Dallas is paved with patios.'

'No, I'm going to let it go wild,' said Sissy. 'Why Dallas?' she repeated, mystified.

'Your work?'

'Not Dallas. But I am a television production assistant. Documentaries mostly. And you?'

'Stockbroker.'

'Thought so,' she said, turning back to her window-cleaning. 'The print-out is written all over you.'

With that remark invading his mind with irritating persistence, Jules returned to London wondering what his new neighbour would be getting up to in his absence. Sissy moved in, lock, stock and video. When he returned for the weekend there were fresh curtains at the windows, flowers in hanging baskets, the brass knocker polished to solar heat proportions, and Sissy having a stereo picnic on her uncut grass.

'Come and have some coffee,' she called out. 'You look whacked.'

'Thank you,' he said, sitting on the grass in his well-cut city suit. Sissy was looking like a peach melba in toning shirt and shorts. 'Was I rude last week? If so, I apologize. It was the unaccustomed . . . racket.'

'Racket? Was there one? I can't remember that far back.' She poured him a mug of coffee from a red enamel coffee pot. She was a mass of contradictions. She looked Dallas, but acted country and western. He didn't know what to make of her.

'Not working?'

'I've taken two weeks leave for moving in,' said Sissy. 'They owe me. We've been chained to the grindstone for the last six months. You don't know how wonderful this is . . . one's own roof after so many hotels and rented places.'

'I've been here a year. It's very quiet and peaceful.' He emphasized the last words slightly, feeling mean. It was her coffee he was drinking. 'Don't you like gardening?'

'It's not that I don't like it. I don't intend to do any. This is going to be a sanctuary,' she explained.

Right on cue, a small boy walked down the path, a cardboard box in his arms. He stopped in front of Sissy.

'Are you the lady who likes hedgehogs?' he asked.

'Yes,' said Sissy, switching off the music.

'I've brought you one,' said the boy. 'I found it wandering round the town. Me Dad said it would die.'

'So it would,' said Sissy, opening the lid of the box. She gasped. Jules looked over her shoulder. It was a comical sight, but pitiful at the same time. The hedgehog had a yoghurt pot stuck over its long pointed nose, impaled on its sharp spines.

'Oh, the poor thing,' said Sissy.

'Strawberry,' said Jules, reading the label. The hedgehog rustled its spines and snuffled inside the pot. 'What a cuddly little creature,' he observed.

'I'll have Cuddles out of that in no time. I'll go indoors and get my scissors. He's probably starving.'

In no time Cuddles was freed from the pot and snuffling towards a dish of steak and kidney pudding, his wet black nose moving like a sensor. He homed in on the food and climbed right into the dish, spreading meat and gravy everywhere.

'Lovely table manners,' said Jules, departing in haste.

'Have you got any spare wire netting?' Sissy asked. 'I want to make an enclosure for her.'

'Her?'

'It's female. I haven't been working on documentaries without learning how to sex a hedgehog.'

Later that evening Jules could hear Sissy hammering his wire netting on to posts. He was trying to watch one of his favourite programmes but the noise was making it impossible.

'That banging is terrible,' he went out and shouted at her.

'I keep missing,' she said, sucking a bruised thumb.

'I'm only doing this for the sake of a quiet evening,' he groaned, taking the hammer from her.

Cuddles took to her new home without much persuasion. It had everything she wanted. A thick hedge into which she could burrow and make a nest for sleeping. An abundant supply of slugs, snails, juicy worms and insects to eat. Restaurant service of bread and milk and the odd tin of dog food were also appreciated. Cuddles began to put on weight, her spines became a glossy creamy-brown.

Sissy brought Cuddles indoors to watch her reaction. The hedgehog took fright, curled up into a ball on the kitchen floor and refused to move for three hours. It took several visits before Cuddles relaxed and started to explore her new environment, clambering over low obstacles in her short-sighted way, not able to skirt round things.

Cuddles was also a consummate escaper. She spent six hours doggedly scratching away at the soil under the wire fencing, only to be returned almost immediately by Jules. It was the third time in three days. Jules carried the hedgehog carefully, wrapped in a towel.

'This is too much,' he said. 'I'm beginning to feel like a taxi service.' Sissy gave him a lovely smile.

'How about coming out with me for dinner next weekend?' suggested Jules suddenly, surprising himself.

'Sorry, but I'd have to be back by ten thirty.'

'Ten thirty? Whatever for?'

'Cuddles's supper. If I'm not here, she might go elsewhere.'

'You mean we'd have to come back for a hedgehog?' Jules could hardly contain his exasperation.

'We could eat here instead,' suggested Sissy. 'I'll cook supper.'

'Stood up for a hedgehog. I'll bring the wine.'

It was a lovely meal. The casserole and Chinese leaf side salad was delicious, the sorbet a dream. And Sissy looked good enough to eat in slim cream pants and a loose pleated blouse, her hair in a crazy top-knot.

Jules longed for a restful evening, finishing off the good claret and drinking coffee, when a weird choking and snorting sound came from the garden. Sissy flew to the back door.

'It's Cuddles,' she cried out. 'Something's happening.'

Jules followed, glass in hand, none too pleased to have their conversation interrupted by a choking hedgehog, but knowing Sissy well enough by now to accept her priorities.

In the gloom, they could just make out the dark shape on the grass that was Cuddles. They then realized that there was not one dark shape but two and the second one was circling Cuddles, making this strange snorting noise. Cuddles was also pivoting round, never taking her eyes off the intruder, every now and then making a snap or a butt as he passed too close.

'Cuddles has a boyfriend,' said Jules.

'Are you sure?' Sissy exclaimed. 'They're such solitary creatures – they don't like the company of other hedgehogs.'

Cuddles's sharp spines were raised in defence. The suitor didn't stand a chance, but he was single-minded and continued his elaborate courtship ceremony.

'You think this is pretty normal behaviour then?' said Sissy dubiously.

'Pretty normal for a hedgehog, I should say,' said Jules, circling Sissy slowly, his eyes on her face. But she was too preoccupied to notice.

'We'd better leave them,' she said, colouring faintly. 'It doesn't seem right to watch.'

'They are a bit like us,' said Jules.

'What do you mean?' said Sissy, prickles rising.

There had already been a degree of defensive circling between them. The city gent often found himself in the garden rattling a dish of food when Sissy was away working; Sissy had agreed to read a leaflet on the value of noise abatement.

She slipped a tape into her music centre. 'Do you mind? Some soft music to drown that appalling noise.'

It was three o'clock in the morning before the snorting ceased. Neither Sissy or Jules had been able to sleep. They were separated by inches, both beds being placed along the dividing wall of the two cottages. Sometimes Sissy imagined she could hear Jules breathing. She sighed deeply. Everything seemed much simpler if you were a hedgehog.

There was nothing to show in the morning except an area of flattened grass. Both hedgehogs had disappeared. But in the evening Cuddles arrived for her supper. Later the second hedgehog appeared, burrowing through the weeds like a small tank. He had found his way in but couldn't find his way out. Cuddles totally ignored him.

'Hello, Oddball,' said Sissy, putting out a second dish. Oddball immediately drew in his muscles and curled into a bristling ball. He stayed still while Cuddles finished his milk.

'This is ridiculous,' said Sissy, grinning. 'Surely you two know each other?'

A few weeks later Sissy had Cuddles on the kitchen scales. 'She's putting on weight,' Sissy told Jules. 'She must be pregnant.'

Jules felt ridiculously pleased. The little creature would occasionally curl up on Sissy's lap. The slugs and snails had disappeared from his garden and he felt sure this was due to Cuddles's insatiable appetite.

'I hope this isn't going to be another noisy event,' said Jules with resignation.

'She'll make a nest,' said Sissy. 'She'll use those sharp spines to comb it into a cosy place for her babies.'

One evening Cuddles wouldn't eat her supper. She waddled away to the nest where she had combed and trampled the dry hay and leaves into a nursery. Jules and Sissy listened to the low snuffling noises coming from the nest under the brambles. Oddball was absent, obviously hunting for his supper.

Jules took Sissy's hand. He wanted desperately to tell her that he cared. How he loved her wild garden; how he loved her shiny Dallas look that hid a tender heart.

'Will she be all right?' asked Sissy, anxiously.

'Give her a little time,' said Jules, holding her hand tightly. 'If she's still snuffling in the morning, we'll get the vet.'

But Cuddles knew how to cope, even if a couple of humans didn't. By morning she was fast asleep, her three babies curled against her furry tummy, their tiny spines soft and white. They were nearly two weeks old before they poked their noses out of the nest to sniff the outside world. Cuddles did not seem to mind when Sissy lifted them up. They made shrill, piping noises in protest.

Jules gave away his lawn mower and moved the wire netting to double the wild garden for the growing population. He did not exactly ask Sissy to marry him; it was rather more a suggestion that the dividing wall was a perfect nuisance and how about knocking it down? Sissy flew into his arms, her eyes like stars.

They noticed a change in their hedgehogs' behaviour as the autumn days grew colder. They seemed to sleep more and forage less. One evening the garden was empty.

Sissy stood calling, rattling the dishes of food, but no small dark mound wandered out of the undergrowth. No small tank bustled through the long grass. No babies followed their mother, wet black noses sweeping the ground.

'They've all gone,' she wept.

Jules held her close. 'Only for the winter, love. They're fast asleep in their cosy nests, living off the fat that your good feeding has helped them to store. And when the spring comes, they'll wake up.'

'But will they come back?'

'Perhaps. But we'll be here and that's what matters.'

A chill wind whipped across the bleak garden, but Sissy was not cold. Another prickly lady had found a cosy nest. And she knew they would both be waiting for when the winter was over and the hedgehogs returned.

THE MAT

The cat sat on the mat. The mat hung on the wall. The wall shook as shells landed on the outskirts of the crumbling, war-torn village. It was the third day of the bombardment and ugly cracks had appeared in the house, like footprints of lightning walking over the whitewashed walls.

Julie huddled under the stout table, holding the cat. It was a striking black tom, called Black Fella for want of a better name. She had found him wandering about in the rubble, disorientated by the fighting and bombing, starved, wild-eyed, growling and hissing at anyone who tried to pick it up.

She had not tried. She loved cats but her job as a television reporter precluded any ownership for the time being. She never knew when she might be sent off to the other end of the world to cover some conflict, some war or natural disaster of immense proportions. It was impossible to have a cat; to always be asking someone to feed it. She did not have those kind of friends.

So she took to carrying cat things around with her on her travels as surrogates. She had a cat brooch and cat earrings (beautiful slim, silver Siamese), a scarf with cute kittens in rows, a big cotton sweatshirt with a fluffy Persian printed on the front. And the mat.

Julie had found the mat in a market in Marakeesh. It was on a junk stall, covered in cobwebs and bits of straw, reeking of stables and dry decay. But Julie saw the embroidered black cat winking at her and the silkiness of his coat shone through all the dirt. She did not even haggle with the trader. The man was old and thin and poor and materially she had everything whereas it was obvious he had very little. She paid what he asked, and the old man's eyes lit up, nodding insanely to himself.

'Where did you get the mat?' she asked him. But he just shrugged, and rolled it up, tying the bundle with a piece of ancient string.

When she found the Black Fella among the rubble, it was his resemblance to her tapestry cat that made her so intent on saving him. Between takes and interviews with soldiers and guerrillas and weeping peasant women who had lost their sons, she left tempting morsels of food close by him, talking, if she had time, in the low, warm and caring voice that had made her reputation on the box.

He came back with her one sleek starless night when the gunfire was still and the soldiers sleeping. The quietness seemed to soothe his ravaged soul and he allowed her to lift him into her arms. She took him to the house, stroking his thin head and talking to him all night. His eyes were strangely green and watched her with a desperate stare.

'I'll look after you,' she said, sharing her supper of corned beef. 'We'll make out, you and I. Don't worry. This war won't go on for ever.'

Black Fella seemed to understand. He slept close to her, and sometimes during that night she felt the softness of his fur brush her skin. In her dreams she thought that the cat that sat on the mat that hung on her wall had come down from its long solitude and was sharing her bed.

Julie did not think about when it would be time to go back to London. She knew she could not just leave the Black Fella, turf him out into the ruined streets to fend for himself. It would be too cruel. But the English quarantine laws . . . would the Black Fella be able to stand the long separation?

She was trying to comb his matted fur when the pain hit her. She held her side till it went away, breathing deeply into the pain as she had been taught. Gradually it swallowed itself and faded away, leaving her dry-mouthed and tired.

They, the great Gods at Guys, could not discover what was the matter with her. She had had tests, X-rays, every possible type of exploratory procedure.

'I'm not going to worry,' she told Black Fella, picking up the comb from the floor. 'One day it'll go away. Pain is only relative after all.'

The cat sat on the mat. The mat hung on the wall. The stone wall reflected a myriad of rainbow light from the flashing sun coming through the alcove. From a distant shore came the sound of lapping waves, too lethargic to do more than stroke the sand in long, lazy curves.

The black cat was curled on an old cushion, breathing

softly and deeply. She dreamed such dreams of long ago, of running through floppy grasses and chasing molten dragon-flies, of a different sea and magnificent cliffs. Her sharp claws curled and uncurled in ecstasy, feeling the tingle of bark along the shaft of nerve ends, smelling the resin from the forest of trees.

Joab fondled the cat's pointed ears with his long brown fingers, his nails raking her skin. It had been a good day. He had dived through the clear water a hundred times, like a fish, dredging the shells from the bed of the Gulf, hauling handfuls of them to the surface.

'We shall eat well tonight, little Yassy,' he said. 'When it's cooler, you and I. But first I have other matters to attend to. I have to see a man of great importance in the village.'

Joab put the pearl in the folds of his brown robe, fastened his sandals and set out along the sandy trail to the cluster of flat-roofed houses near the well. The merchant would be there at dusk to buy from the divers. He would like to own the divers, pay them a weekly wage and keep all the pearls. But Joab preferred to work for himself. He had always worked the sea alone. He had no intention of changing, though he knew odd rumours were in the air. They had found thick liquid gold under the sand and soon there would be machines pumping it up from the desert and it would bring great wealth to everyone. He did not believe it.

'Ahlan wa sahlan.'

'Ahlan beek.'

'Masa il-khair.'

'Masa in-nur.'

'So what have you for me, Joab?' said the merchant from the shadows, the formal courtesies over. His face was very dark, his corded agal at a rakish angle, his kaffiyeh the traditional red check fabric. A young woman covered her face, but there was no disguising her flashing eyes. The sound of the wooden water-wheels creaked through Joab's head and he forgot what he had come to say.

'Come, come, don't keep me waiting.'

'I have a pearl, m'effendiah. A pearl for a sheikh, a prince, fit for a king.'

'Show me.'

Joab hesitated. He did not trust the merchant or the young woman who peered at him from the doorway. He only wanted to sell the pearl and go back to his home close to the sea. Yassy would be waiting for him. He was always afraid that she might run away or be stolen if he was gone too long. No one had ever stayed in his life and the cat filled a great void.

'Show me, fool!'

Joab brought out the pearl. It glistened in the palm of his hand like a small globe, the iridescence flowing from it in waves of light. It was not only milky but faintly pink, as if touched by the fingers of dawn.

He heard the woman gasp, felt her greed swallowing the air. The pearl was not for her. If the merchant paid good money it would lay on the throat of a princess or adorn the finger of an Arab prince.

The offer was reluctant and miserably small. Joab was not a fool. He knew the pearl had greater value. He shook his head.

'La, la,' he said. 'It is not enough.'

'Itfaddal!' the merchant shrieked as Joab put the pearl back into his robe. 'Imshi!'

Joab let the merchant's annoyance wash over his head. He bowed politely and walked back to his isolated stone dwelling. The Qur'an said that all bartering should be fair and he had not been offered the worth of the pearl.

'Ma'alesh,' he said to his cat as they shared a supper of freshly baked fish. 'It doesn't matter.'

He straightened the mat that hung on the wall, winking back at the silken cat. His parents had left him the mat. It was his inheritance. He would never sell it, even if the time came when his lungs were too weak to dive.

But the next day when he was diving in the clear Arabian water, the merchant and the woman came to his home and searched everywhere for the pearl. When they found it, hidden in the intricate stitching of the mat, Yassy jumped on the merchant's shoulder and dug her claws into his neck. He screamed and pulled her off and the woman kicked Yassy in the ribs, thinking this might earn her the pearl – but it didn't.

Even as Yassy licked and licked at her broken rib, the pearl was being passed on its way through greasy hands in the great web of merchandise that stretched towards the avarice of men.

Joab did not weep for the pearl. But he wept for Yassy and touched her gently, for every movement made her mouth dry with pain and he could not understand why anyone should hurt such a small creature.

He made her lay in the sunshine and the warmth healed her injuries, but he never again found a pearl so large or so beautiful.

The dredgers came to dig a port for the tankers and Joab watched in astonishment from the dunes as they excavated deeply into the ocean bed. Their monster mouths tore out great hauls of shells and sand, tossing them back in cascades of light. He did not realize they were devastating his livelihood. He did not know that one day he would even have to sell the mat to survive.

The cold winter wind tore over the Yorkshire moors as if possessed by the devil. Emily Jane walked over the rough terrain, her funereal black skirts flapping, holding on to her bonnet with one hand, the other clutching her shawl. Her sisters had told her not to walk that day, but she had to go out. The parsonage was suffocating her.

There had been so many funerals. And the next would be hers. She knew that. The sky told her. The clouds wrote her name across the sky, stretched in wisps of vapour so that only she could read it. The rain pattered a stinging message on her face. She was not afraid. She welcomed death, even more than life. She did not want to cope with life.

Blackie ran beside her. He was black from tip to toe, vigorous and lively, making up for what the sisters lacked in playfulness and pranks. He loved all the sisters equally but knew that he did not have long to be with Emily. He knew, because he recognized her fragile hold.

Emily cherished her life on the moors; the isolated hill hamlets were grey with loneliness. The blunt air was harsh on her weakened lungs and sometimes her breath rasped with pain but the force of her character took no notice of such inconvenience. If she wanted to walk on the moors, then walk she would. She did not want a poisoning doctor telling her what she could do and what she could not. Nor would she take his potions or pills.

Her cough and cold were obstinate and the pain in her chest made breathing difficult. She had got so thin that her clothes hung like sackcloth.

'I shall leave in haste,' she told the cat as he ambled beside her, tail high like a plume. 'I have no wish to linger on this cold earth. If the task of dying lays before me, then I shall tell my spirit to meet this fate with all temerity. I have no pity for myself; only bitterness to leave what is undone, undone. I know there is so much more within me. Oh Blackie . . .' And she scooped the cat up into her arms. 'When shall I see these wild hills again? Where has my youth gone?'

He scampered across the bracken and purple heather, exhilarated by the wind, his tail streaming, feathering the fern. Then he remembered and returned, rubbing his head against her worn black boot.

'I must drive on with my work,' she said, burying her face in his soft fur. 'I must not be idle.'

Thus she wrote in her small hand the words that rang of love and lust and passion, while her skin burned of fever and her wasted frame stumbled in spirit over the rough ground.

But she drooped and sickened. Keeper, her fierce and faithful bulldog, stayed by her couch stretched on a mat, but Blackie could not stay. He had to run the wild moors. He ran for Emily, bringing back the scent of bracken in his fur and dewdrops like diamonds hanging from his whiskers.

It was late December as the frost gripped the moor in an icy shiver when Emily escaped. In the end, she went swiftly. Keeper suffered and howled. But Blackie ran with the wind, taking her spirit with him to the top of the wild, bleak moors where she would always be free.

The cat sat on the mat. The mat hung newly on the wall to honour her husband, Sir Rob Huish, soon to return from defeating the great Spanish Armada. Genevieve put the last stitches into the tapestry, tidying a thread here and there, kissing the sweet face of the black silk cat.

'He will be home soon,' she whispered, smiling. 'Safe and home. And you are my gift to him.'

She remembered the night that the fire beacons had been lit all along the coast of South Devon. One by one the points of light blazed from the clifftops, alerting the Devonians that the invincible fleet of Spanish ships was sailing up the English Channel. Genevieve had known that her sailor husband would rally immediately to the English Fleet under Lord Howard of Effingham. His Devon farm could fend for itself while he was away.

'My dearest Geney,' he had whispered, holding her close. 'I hate to go, but I must for the sake of our son, for the sake of England.'

Genevieve could barely speak. This handsome, raven-haired man was the centre of her universe. She lived for his every word, his warm embraces, his breath upon her skin. How lucky she was to love and adore her young husband, and to be loved in return. Her sisters were locked in loveless marriages to older men, married off for political reasons.

But Genevieve and Rob had married for love, despite all the parental arguments. Being the youngest of three sisters, Genevieve brought little dowry and no lands.

'It is only you that I want,' he said, carrying her away to a warm, steaming hayloft in the bitter, snow-bound winter of 1586. 'I don't care if you bring a pig or a poke. My mind is made up.'

'But your farms need money,' she protested, so very lightly. 'You should marry a wealthy widow.'

'This is the only wealth I'll ever take,' he said, burying

his face in her glossy dark hair, his breath laboured as he fought to contain his desire.

That spring Genevieve ran through the floppy grasses of the soft Devon meadows, barefoot on the rust-coloured soil, chasing the molten dragonflies. She was so happy. At last her parents could not hold back their consent, and she and Rob were married in good time for their son to be born in wedlock.

But there were rumours and rumblings of Philip II's determination to strike a blow against England. They heard of a gigantic naval fleet being built, over 130 ships with heavy guns.

Genevieve could not paint or draw but she could sew. A portrait of her handsome husband was out of the question, so instead she began a tapestry of a cat, a cat with fur the colour of Rob's raven hair and the same twinkle in his bright blue eyes.

'I shall finish it for your return,' she said, crushing her tears with an iron will. He must go to fight the Armada with only her smile in his heart.

Rob kissed her, then his little son, then put his hand on the flank of the silken tapestry cat. 'This is my promise that I will return from the fighting.'

And he kept his promise. Genevieve heard that so many of the enemy ships were damaged that they could not make the journey home and had sailed for Dunkirk. The English Fleet were coming home. She hung the finished tapestry on the stone wall so that it would be the first thing that Rob would see as he came in. The dining hall was far from draught-proof and the tapestry swung in the strong wind that gusted from outside. A southwesterly storm was gathering force, waves crashing against the spectacular cliffs.

Genevieve listened to the howling gale, fear in her heart. 'Is there news?' she asked as a servant hurried in, ashen-faced.

'A Spanish galleon is being driven ashore near Hope Cove. It's a hospital ship, they say, with many wounded men aboard, and no one strong enough to sail her. Sir Rob has gone to help bring it in.'

'No,' she cried. 'Not Rob. He must come home.'

Pulling a thick shawl round her shoulders, she ran out into the storm, slipping on the wet earth, the rain stinging her face. She climbed, breath pinned to a stitch in her side, to Bolt Tail where she could see down into the mist-shrouded cove. Among the pounding seas the great masted ship creaked and floundered in distress. Through the spray she could just make out its name, the *San Pedro el Mayor*.

She ran down the path towards Hope, longing for sight of a tall man with thick raven hair. Her breath came fast, heart pounding, her hair streaming from its pins in the wind.

Then she saw him, being carried ashore through the furious waves by two stalwart sailors; all were drenched. His body was broken, crushed between the rocks and the hull of the wrecked ship. There was no life in it. His proud head fell back, his hair plastered like strands of black silk across a face which bore no resemblance to her Rob.

Distraught, she threw herself into the sea and a great wave lifted her and flung her against a jagged and glistening slab of rock. A pain tore into her side and the cry that came from her mouth went echoing endlessly into the future.

'There is nothing, absolutely nothing at all to account for this pain,' said the consultant, putting down the file of notes, tests and X-rays. 'You're a very fit young woman. A little tired, perhaps . . .'

'You mean it's a phantom pain?' asked Julie. 'That I'm imagining it?'

'No, I'm not suggesting that you imagine it. I'm sure it's very real indeed. But it could be a phantom pain. After an amputation, a patient often feels pain in the limb that isn't there any more.'

Julie shuddered. 'So the pain could be in a part of my body that doesn't exist?' It was a bewildering thought.

The consultant looked confused. 'Perhaps you could do a television programme on it . . .'

She let herself into her London flat, resolved that this was the last time she would try to find out what was the matter with her. Black Fella stood up and stretched lazily. He had been sitting on top of the microwave, his favourite perch. He was looking good, months of regular food and care had given his coat a healthy sheen.

He jumped down to welcome her home. Julie went on to her knees to run her fingers through his fur. He was the only thing she had managed to save when the mortar bombs hit the house. She had fled from the oncoming tanks, leaving everything behind, even the mat.

The cat sat on the mat. The mat hung on a wall. Another wall, a different wall, a wall from which the silken cat could watch and wait . . .

Home Life With Cats

Brian Aldiss
Illustrated by Karin van Heerden

Home Life With Cats is a collection of thirty-four poems by Brian Aldiss, and a unique celebration of cats he has known and loved.

Beautifully illustrated by Karin van Heerden, it is a treasury of feline delight from one of Britain's most renowned writers.

'I challenge anyone who has ever owned a cat not to respond instantly to these delightful poems'

Desmond Morris (from the Introduction)

ISBN 0 586 21428 3

A Cat is Watching
A Look at the Way Cats See Us

Roger A. Caras

As anyone who shares a home with a cat will know, all cats are watchers, observing us as we go about our daily business and perhaps understanding us in a way we cannot comprehend. Now, in this warm and fascinating book by an acknowledged cat expert, we can turn the tables and look at the world from *their* perspective.

In an irresistible blend of biology, cat-psychology and personal experience, Roger Caras provides us with a cat's-eye view of life that will give all cat lovers an intriguing new insight into the behaviour of their pets.

ISBN 0 586 21718 5